GRIMM REAPERS

MICHAEL E. BERG

120
pages

Printed in the United States of America

First Printing, 2017

ISBN-10: 1-947197-08-8
ISBN-13: 978-1-947197-08-4

120pages
Subway Sites LLC
PO BOX 231548
New York, NY 10023

120pages.com

HOW TO READ A SCREENPLAY

A screenplay is written to show, not tell. Screenplays convey how a film will play out. The story unfolds through the dialogue and actions of the characters. As such, words are used economically. There is less description than you would find in a novel, as those details are typically handled during the production process. There is very little exposition; the screenplay doesn't provide any information that an audience watching the film wouldn't receive.

Therefore, as you read, visualize a film in your mind and "see" it as if you were watching a film.

If you're not familiar with the screenplay format, here are some things to know:

SCENE HEADINGS

Scene headings describe where the action takes place, the time of day, and sometimes additional details, such as if the action takes place in a flashback or as part of a montage.

For example:

```
INT. SAMMY'S HOUSE - DAY
```

"INT" indicates the action is indoors. "SAMMY'S HOUSE" tells us the action is in a woman's house. "DAY" tells us that it is daytime.

```
EXT. PARK - NIGHT
```

"EXT" indicates the action is outdoors. "PARK" tells us we are in a park. "NIGHT" tells us that it is the evening.

Other time descriptions may be used, such as "SAME" to indicate action taking place simultaneously or "LATER" to indicate action taking place moments later, after a brief jump in time.

CAPITALIZED WORDS

Throughout a screenplay, you may come across CAPITALIZED WORDS. These generally indicate the introduction of a new character, that the camera should pay attention to a particular item/sound/person/location, or that we are moving into a specific place within the location.

For example:

```
John turns.  He sees SALLY, the most beautiful girl he has ever
laid eyes on.  In her hands, she holds AN ADORABLE PUPPY.
```

DIALOGUE

Dialogue is written by centering a character's name with their spoken words appearing beneath their name. For example:

```
                    JOHN
          You found Charlie!
```

PARANTHETICALS

Between the character's name and dialogue, you may see text in parenthesis. This indicates some specific direction about how the dialogue is to be read or some specific action that takes place during the delivery of the dialogue.

```
                    JOHN
              (eyes watering)
          You found Charlie!
```

OTHER TERMS

Here are some other terms you may come across when reading a screenplay:

(O.S.) or (O.C.) – Off-screen or off-camera indicates that we do not see a character when dialogue is heard

(V.O.) – Indicates voiceover. This is dialogue we hear, but the speaker is not physically present in the same location as the action

(CONT'D) – Indicates that the same character is continuing to deliver a line of dialogue after an action, scene change, or page break

(MORE) – Indicates that the dialogue from the character continues on the next page

POV – Indicates that we see the action through a defined point of view

SUPERIMPOSE – Indicates that we see text on screen, often to define a time or location

MONTAGE – Indicates rapid cutting of different scenes in a sequence, such as any training sequence in a Rocky movie

(beat) – Indicates that a character takes a brief pause before continuing dialogue

For Crystal

The one who stole my heart with her own breathtaking intensity.

Your support through the years has meant the world to me.

FADE IN:

EXT. BERLIN - HUMBOLDT UNIVERSITY - DAY

A picturesque afternoon. Horse-drawn carriages rattle along a
cobblestone street outside iron gates surrounding the former
palace.

SUPERIMPOSE: "Berlin, Humboldt University, 1861"

ONLOOKERS in top hats and petticoats mingle around the
formidable statue of Frederick the Great.

INT. HUMBOLDT UNIVERSITY - HALLWAY

STUDENTS bustle between classes.

The din fades away farther down near a forgotten door affixed
with the brass nameplate: "J. GRIMM."

INT. CLASSROOM

Amid the clutter of books and papers, JACOB GRIMM, 76,
hunched over in a dusty frock coat, writes with quiet
concentration etched across his haggard face.

He replaces the parchment with a new sheet.

The quill tip scratches out fresh words: "My Dearest Herman,"
--

                    JACOB (V.O.)
          My dearest Herman. I hope this
          letter finds you and Gisela well.
          My time remains regulated by an
          endeavor that is beyond measure.
          Progress on the dictionary has
          slowed to a snail's pace.

He contemplates a framed 1812 etching of him and Wilhelm.

                    JACOB (V.O.)
          Your father's passing has left a
          great void these past two years.
          Not only was he my brother but
          closest friend. This is why,
          nephew, before death ensues, I
          impart one last story. A tale never
          meant for publication, but one you
          deserve to know.

The quill pen dips into an inkwell...

INT. CASTLE LICHTENSTEIN - BIRTH CHAMBER - DAY

...lifts back up, but now held by the palace RECORD KEEPER.

He glimpses from feverish scrawling at the LABORED DELIVERY of DUCHESS AUGUSTA, 23, an endearing yet battered wife, surrounded by HANDMAIDENS.

Augusta screams in agony on a parturition chair.

SUPERIMPOSE: "Castle Lichtenstein, 1788"

Her legs are spread on wooden stirrups: sweat and blood dripping in unison.

One handmaiden dabs Augusta's forehead with a wet cloth while a NUN squats in front. Augusta cries out in a low moan...

...that turns pleasurable inside the ROYAL BED CHAMBER. An opulent den of gilded furnishings, and alabaster sculptures on opposite marble fireplaces.

A celestial ceiling mural overlooks blue bed linens where a MISTRESS, ageless beauty, gyrates on top of FREDERICK I, 34, a behemoth 6'11", 400 lb prince.

Her silky hair flows down over flawless skin and supple curves to the meaty hands caressing her buttocks.

INTERCUT DUCHESS/MISTRESS MONTAGE

An escalation of delivery torment and sexual indulgence until both climax in a twisted duality.

END MONTAGE

INT. BIRTH CHAMBER

A melancholy mood. Blood-stained handmaidens look lost in ways to comfort the Duchess as she cries on her bed.

The Nun cradles a swaddled, silent INFANT. She shakes her head to the Record Keeper.

INT. ROYAL BED CHAMBER

The Mistress wraps in a lavish robe that complements her allure. She drapes herself over the satisfied noble.

> MISTRESS
> How may I pleasure my prince now?

                    FREDERICK
          By restraining your incessant
          urges. Go fetch me a drink.

The doors burst open. A host of GUARDS march in with swords
drawn.

Frederick sits up.

                    FREDERICK
          How dare you. Get out!

The GUARD CAPTAIN approaches, holding Augusta: staggering,
overwrought, clothes bled through.

                    GUARD CAPTAIN
          Seize that woman!

Two guards wrench the Mistress off of Frederick.

                    FREDERICK
          I demand an answer to this outrage.

                    AUGUSTA
               (labored)
          Your deceptive harlot is a witch!
          She's stolen more than my bed.

The Guard Captain struggles at keeping Augusta upright.

                    MISTRESS
          Lies, my prince. I only wish to
          serve.

                    AUGUSTA
          Look, look upon your son.

She collapses. Handmaidens rush to her side.

The Nun brings forth the stillborn baby. Frederick gazes at
his dead offspring...

                    MISTRESS (O.S.)
          Frederick, please. I love you.

...then to the Mistress.

His flustered face contorts into rage.

                    FREDERICK
          Burn her!

EXT. CASTLE LICHTENSTEIN - COURTYARD

A crowd of PEASANTS gather as guards lead the Mistress to a
scorched WOODEN PYRE and bind her hands behind the charred
center pole.

They douse the pyre with oil.

The Mistress shifts her shoulders and the robe falls off,
exposing her breasts. She gazes up at the CASTLE BALCONY
where Frederick stands.

He glances back at a pool of blood on his bedroom floor. Then
nods down to the Guard Captain holding a flaming torch.

                    GUARD CAPTAIN
          By order of his majesty, Prince of
          Württemberg, I condemn thee to
          death.

                    MISTRESS
          A slanderous betrayal, my lord.
          Spare me and I shall be yours.

Her words are hypnotic, verbal honey: several guards appear
entranced.

                    GUARD CAPTAIN
          Stay true, men. She's salacious and
          vile. Send this enchantress to the
          burning depths.

He casts his torch down, flames erupt.

                    MISTRESS
          Not by your hand, or his.

She projects her defiance to the balcony and cackles. Her
shrill laughter intensifies with the blaze.

Smooth skin wrinkles like a raisin. Perky breasts sag and
shrivel.

A guard vomits.

The Mistress doesn't perish but reveals her true, abhorrent
self: a 174-year-old Slavic witch named BABA YAGA. She casts
a spell.

                    BABA YAGA
          Oheň viac ma lietať!

The fire crystallizes and forms a gigantic GLASS MORTAR.

Everyone falls back in fear.

Baba Yaga launches her mortar up into the overcast sky.

Frederick watches with despair, not even phased by the sight of snow...

EXT. GRIMM HOUSE - DAY

...falling gently on an idyllic German residence and backyard that borders entrance to deep woods.

SUPERIMPOSE: "Steinau, January 10, 1796"

CRACK! An AXE blade splits a piece of wood.

PHILIPP GRIMM, 44, a hardy man with tender eyes and temperament, shimmies the blade off the chopping block. He glances over at --

JACOB, 11, cocking back the trigger of a CROSSBOW and handing it to his brother WILHELM, 10.

                    PHILIPP
          Take a deep breath, Will. Steady
          your aim.

The crossbow sights line up on a crudely painted bullseye hanging off a branch.

Wilhelm releases the bolt -- SCHTING! It ricochets off the tree trunk.

                    JACOB
               (snickers)
          Just a tad off the mark.

                    WILHELM
          Not again! This is hopeless,
          Father. I'll never hit it.

                    PHILIPP
          Chin up, you've only just begun.

                    JACOB
          Let's try a bigger target: troll-
          size!

Philipp furrows his brow in disapproval. Picks up the bolt.

                    PHILIPP
          Over here, Jacob. Come retrieve
          this for your brother.

                    JACOB
          Why, Father?

Philipp remains silent as he readies a new wood chunk.

Wilhelm grins, sticks out his tongue. Jacob snatches the
crossbow from him and marches over in a huff.

                    PHILIPP
          Try not to mock Wilhelm, it
          disheartens him.

                    JACOB
          He's too sensitive. Can't take a
          good ribbing.

                    PHILIPP
          Always remember your place as the
          oldest and the responsibility it
          entails. I shan't be around forever.

Philipp brings the axe down. CRACK!

                    MOTHER (O.S.)
          Philipp? Philipp?

Jacob spots his MOTHER leaning out of an upper-story window.

                    MOTHER
          Bring the boys inside before you
          catch the death of cold.

She shuts the window and disappears from view.

                    PHILIPP
              (to Wilhelm)
          That's enough for today. Do as your
          mother has requested.

                    WILHELM
          Yes, Father.

He trudges his way around front.

                    PHILIPP
          I'm counting on you, Jacob, to be
          provider and protector of this
          family when the time comes.

The wind picks up, blowing the snow harder. Jacob shields his
face.

HOWLING rises above the bluster.

                         PHILIPP
                Get inside.

He yanks his axe free. Focuses on the forest.

                         JACOB
                      (hesitates)
                What is it, Father?

Philipp scans the area... snaps his attention to --

A monstrous WEREWOLF leaping into view!

                         PHILIPP
                Go! Now!

He charges with his axe raised. The Werewolf growls as it
stands on two legs, looming over --

Philipp who swings the axe multiple times until cutting
across the beast's chest.

The Werewolf pounces, snapping like a rabid dog; Philipp jams
the axe handle between its jaws.

Jacob trembles as he tries to load the crossbow.

The Werewolf clamps onto the handle and flings it away --
THWUMP! It lurches back, shoulder pierced by a bolt.

Philipp flips over, starts to crawl.

                         PHILIPP
                Jacob... run!

The Werewolf swipes its claw across Philipp's back, ripping
into flesh.

                         JACOB
                FATHER!

He fumbles reloading.

                         WILHELM (O.S.)
                Jacob? Mother waits for --

Wilhelm peeks his head around the corner and gasps.

Sharp, jagged teeth tear a chunk out of Philipp's neck.

Philipp gasps for air, clutching the wound as blood seeps
through his fingers.

Jacob aims the crossbow...

The Werewolf snarls then lunges!

...and shoots.

The creature slumps into the snow, dead -- a bolt sunk in its forehead -- transforms back to a naked YOUNG MAN.

Jacob's in shock but moves past, inching up to Philipp. Stops just short of the expanding red snow.

GURGLE-GLUT -- Philipp struggles to pull something from his jacket. Chokes out one last breath and dies.

Through a blurry vision of tears, Jacob notices a shiny object in his father's hand.

Jacob kneels down and plucks out a GOLDEN KEY.

INT. PALACE - DRAWING ROOM - DAY

The key hangs on a chain around the neck of JACOB, 25, introspective face with short, wavy hair in a formal suit befitting a meager salary.

WILHELM, 24, longer hair parted, more jovial and carefree attitude, flirts with a BOUFFANT LADY nearby.

SUPERIMPOSE: "Napoleonshöhe, Kingdom of Westphalia, 1810"

They are surrounded by extravagance, tapestries, and LADIES OF COURT: gossip and giggling accompany their generous consumption of champagne.

Jacob has a quill pen to parchment, writing until --

> JACOB
> R-U-M-P-E-L...

He looks to QUEEN CATHARINA, 27, round face, tight hanging curls, dressed in the finest Prussian linens.

> JACOB
> Once more, please.

> CATHARINA
> S-T-I, L-T-S, KIN: Rumpelstiltskin.

> JACOB
> And that's how the queen saved her
> child.

> CATHARINA
> Recounted by my family for
> generations.

                    WILHELM
          I find it peculiar the imp should
          fly out on a cooking ladle.

                    CATHARINA
          He must be very tiny.

                    JACOB
          Or the ladle belonged to a giant.

Catharina laughs along with her sister-in-law PRINCESS
CHARLOTTE, 23, a homely girl with tired eyes.

                    CATHARINA
          Warms my heart to see Charlotte's
          spirits lifted.

She gives an encouraging grin to Charlotte.

                    CHARLOTTE
          A welcomed respite from
          recent...events... forgive me.

She averts her eyes, begins to cry.

Jacob fidgets from the awkwardness. Wilhelm interjects.

                    WILHELM
          May I say what an honor it's been
          spending the afternoon with such
          lovely company. Supplies my brother
          a much needed distraction from his
          royal library duty.

Catharina signals to an ATTENDANT...

                    CATHARINA
          Return the princess to her
          chambers.

...who leads Charlotte away.

                    JACOB
          I apologize, my queen, if we
          offended in some manner.

                    CATHARINA
          The poor thing's been anguished
          since her infant son succumbed to
          consumption. Our doctors say such
          despair is caused by a brain fever.

                    JACOB
          Prone to delusions?

                         CATHARINA
               Yes, and nightmares. Nursing a
               demon child or some such nonsense.

The brothers exchange intrigued looks.

                         WILHELM
               If it pleases, m'lady, may I offer
               a Bavarian root tonic? Used to
               bring deep sleep for troubled
               nights.

                         CATHARINA
               Is it safe?

                         WILHELM
               I always keep a vial near my
               bedside.

Wilhelm sidles up to the Bouffant Lady with a new glass of
champagne.

                         JACOB
               Perhaps it's time we take our
               leave.

               WILHELM   BOUFFANT LADY
So soon?   So soon?

                         CATHARINA
               You mustn't depart until I share my
               last tale.

                         WILHELM
               Yes, dear brother. It'd be
               improper, immoral, and impolite to
               deny the queen.

He declares while locking eyes with the enamored Bouffant
Lady.

Jacob dips the quill.

                         JACOB
               Please continue.

                         CATHARINA
               When I was a little girl, a servant
               accused of witchery was to be
               executed. However, she escaped my
               father's castle...

EXT. BLACK FOREST - DAY - FLASHBACK (1788)

An A-FRAME HUT with a mossy roof barges through the trees on
gargantuan CHICKEN LEGS and nestles itself on a cleared
embankment.

> CATHARINA (V.O.)
> ...and fled south, deep into the
> Black Forest as the royal guard lay
> pursuit.

A company of ROYAL GUARD gallop into view.

The Guard Captain signals his troops to dismount and draw
their swords. All cautiously advance except for one.

Chicken Leg Hut's oval doorway opens like a mouth, causing
them to hesitate when --

A line of sharpened posts burst from the ground, IMPALING
three guards!

The ten-foot wall blocks remainder from escape.

The lone guard stands helpless as SCREAMS of torment and
death erupt from the other side.

Once the slaughter subsides, a bloodied burlap sack sails
over the wall and lands at his feet.

> BABA YAGA (O.S.)
> A present for your prince. Deliver
> as a warning to all with ill
> intentions, lest they wish the same
> fate.

INT. PALACE - DRAWING ROOM - DAY (1810)

Bouffant Lady leans forward, almost falling off her chair.

> BOUFFANT LADY
> What was inside?

> CATHARINA
> The captain's head.

> JEROME (O.S.)
> Absurde.

Everyone rises as KING JEROME BONAPARTE, 26, enters, dressed
a little more regal than he needs to match his ego.

                    JEROME
          I'm surprised, my dear, to hear
          such nonsense leave your lips.

                    CATHARINA
          My father saw the head.

                    JEROME
          Then he ought to have strung up
          that guard for murder and
          desertion.

                    JACOB
          It's a captivating story regardless
          of veracity.

                    CATHARINA
          The witch also killed my mother.

Jacob shares a knowing glance with Wilhelm.

                    WILHELM
          Our deepest of sympathies, m'lady.

Jerome joins Catharina on the decorative sofa.

                    JACOB
          No one should be burdened to carry
          such a tragedy gone unanswered.

He catches the slightest admittance of sorrow pass over
Catharina's face. She snaps back into her facade of regal
aloofness before Jerome notices.

                    CATHARINA
          I left my past back in Lichtenstein.
          Old memories have no place here.

                    JEROME
          And neither do old wives' tales.
          Now let us not forget social graces
          befitting a king. Who sits before
          me?

                    WILHELM
          Wilhelm, my liege, honored to be in
          your presence.

                    JACOB
          My brother recently returned from
          his travels to Weimar.

                    WILHELM
          Researching local legends and oral
          narratives.

                    JEROME
          To what end?

                    JACOB
          A belief that one day the provinces
          will unite as a single state. After
          our land is purged of unspoken
          evils --

                    WILHELM
               (interrupts)
          -- into written form. So all may
          embrace a common German heritage.

Jerome studies Jacob long enough to be uncomfortable.

                    JEROME
          Be careful how you phrase these
          noble, if not pointless, endeavors.
          Duller minds may mistake them as
          treason.

He stands up and wanders to a large window overlooking the
expansive grounds.

                    JEROME
          Only Napoleon can achieve a
          European union. My brother shall
          build an empire grander than Rome.

INT. PALACE - BEDROOM - NIGHT

Jacob and Wilhelm creep into the dimly lit room, armed for
battle. Long-stem candles glow off ornate woodwork.

MOANING and SUCKING sounds drift from behind a finely woven
bed curtain.

                    WILHELM
          Wait. Are you sure? Whatever lies
          beyond that curtain --

                    JACOB
          Has already been revealed, fourteen
          years ago. We can't turn a blind
          eye now. This is our path to
          follow.

Wilhelm nods, and they step closer when a horse SNORT brings
new confusion. Jacob draws back the curtain --

Exposing pale eyes of a floating horse head. The ghostly
NIGHT MARE peeks out from a dream veil.

An ALP, small humanoid creature with a lengthy tail and soot-
colored fur, nurses from the exposed Princess Charlotte.

                    JACOB
              (aghast)
          Myth realized as abomination.

The Alp raises its head and bares fangs from a grotesque,
milky squirrel-face.

                    WILHELM
          Repulsive little imp, isn't he.

Bat wings and horns sprout from the Alp's body.

                    JACOB
          The Night Mare must be its conduit.
              (aims PISTOL CROSSBOW)
          Let's be quick.

Wilhelm ducks as the Alp launches into the air.

It flaps around, uncoordinated like a baby bird, knocking
over candles: one sets fire to a bed curtain.

Jacob douses the flame with a wash basin.

The Alp crashes into a fruit bowl on the dinner table. Begins
pelting the brothers with apples, oranges, and lemons.

Wilhelm unsheathes his early 18th century RAPIER and slices
through the barrage of produce.

An orange chunk spooks the Night Mare onto the physical plane
-- bumping Wilhelm over as it enters.

                    WILHELM
          This complicates matters.

The Alp goes airborne, buffering itself behind the horse.

                    JACOB
          We mustn't let the Alp ride back
          into the netherworld.

Wilhelm rips down the burnt bed curtain and holds it out like
a net.

They press forward from opposite sides. The Night Mare
obstructs Jacob who pets it out of happenstance.

Wilhelm lunges, tossing the heavy curtain. The Alp dodges and flies over to a nightstand.

Jacob turns, fires his pistol crossbow --

A mirror cracks as the Alp squeaks, dropping to the floor.

White fluid leaks from its torso.

Jacob rushes over, scooping up a lemon wedge and crams it in the flailing creature's mouth: instantly subdued.

Wilhelm shuffles closer, wheezing, gasping for composure...

                    WILHELM
          Pain, in chest.

                    JACOB
          It's really not the time.

...regains control with a final gulp of air.

                    WILHELM
          Some brotherly love. What if I had
          heart failure or a collapsed lung?

                    JACOB
          A refreshing change from your other
          fictitious ailments.

Jacob holds out his hand. Wilhelm grasps it with a comforting shake.

                    JACOB
          Sword.

Wilhelm relinquishes the swept-hilt handle.

Jacob positions himself over the paralyzed Alp as though he were about to tee off.

                    JACOB
          Death comes for us all, creature. I
          am yours, I am Death.

He lops off the Alp's head. Milk pours from the open cavity until its body DECOMPOSES into nothingness.

                    WILHELM
          Good work and good riddance.

The Night Mare neighs at Jacob then laps up the puddle.

Charlotte stirs in her sleep.

16.

Jacob runs a hand over the horse's soft, glistening coat.

                    JACOB
          This remarkable beast could simply
          disappear when the princess awakes.

Wilhelm wipes clean his rapier and sheathes it. He surveys
the room's destruction.

                    WILHELM
          I rather not be here when either
          happens.

Jacob loops a length of curtain cord around the horse's neck
and leads it out.

Wilhelm retrieves the bolt before following.

                    JACOB (O.S.)
          We may need a story for my new
          friend.

                    WILHELM (O.S.)
          A gift from her majesty for
          services rendered.

EXT. KASSEL - PALACE - MORNING

Dressed in travel cloaks, the brothers secure last of their
gear to the Night Mare and Wilhelm's stallion: outfitted for
a long journey.

                    WILHELM
          I'm glad more attention was on
          Princess Charlotte's recovery than
          her room.

                    JACOB
          Still, we shouldn't linger here a
          moment beyond our needs.

A carriage rolls up the palace entrance ramp.

ACHIM VON ARNIM, 29, literary celebrity with a baby face and
pouty lips, opens the carriage door.

                    ACHIM
          It can't be. My two favorite
          scholars waiting for me?

He skips down the steps and embraces both of them.

                    WILHELM
          Achim, what a pleasant surprise.

                    ACHIM
          I thought it might, but I'm sad to
          see you aren't staying. Off to
          collect more folktales?

                    JACOB
          Conducting business on the queen's
          behalf.

                    ACHIM
          Exactly why I'm here. Personally
          summoned to read from the third
          volume of *Des Knaben Wunderhorn*.

                    WILHELM
          She'll be a captive audience.

                    ACHIM
          A pity Brentano isn't here to soak
          up her praise. Which reminds me,
          have any new pages ready? He's
          eager for more.

                    JACOB
          Our collection only numbers a
          couple dozen.

                    ACHIM
          The quantity bears no concern. I'd
          be happy to pass along whatever you
          possess.

Jacob lifts the flap of a leather SATCHEL and pulls out a
stack of parchment. He gives them to Achim.

                    ACHIM
          Favor me this request, Jacob. Delay
          your departure by a few hours. Let
          us discuss what future awaits the
          Brothers Grimm.

EXT. BAD WILDUNGEN - NIGHT

Jacob and Wilhelm travel along a muddy route flanked by
trees.

                    WILHELM
          I thought Achim's ideas for being
          published were very captivating.

                    JACOB
          His enthusiasm was infectious but
          nothing of particular importance.

                    WILHELM
          You could have tried appearing
          interested.

                    JACOB
                  (irritable)
          Our pretense as story collectors
          holds nothing beyond its purpose.
          Don't ask of me any more than
          needed towards this falsehood.

They remain silent for the next several minutes while Jacob
dispels his guilt from spouting off.

                    WILHELM
          Why are we meeting Marie in Bad
          Wildungen?

                    JACOB
          There's no town nearer to her
          grandmother's cottage.

Wilhelm observes several skeletons dangling by their neck.

                    WILHELM
          And none more hospitable I'm sure.

EXT. BAD WILDUNGEN - SENTRY TOWER

They stop before a high wooden gate extended out from a solid
wall encircling the town. A FRENCH SOLDIER peers down from
his lookout.

                    JACOB
          Good evening, sir. We wish to
          enter.

The French Soldier yells back behind him.

          FRENCH SOLDIER   SUBTITLE
Chiens errants prussiens   Stray Prussian dogs come
viennent aboyer à notre   barking at our gate.
porte.

          JACOB   SUBTITLE
Qui posséder manières fines   Who possess finer manners
que la tour troll.   than the tower troll.

The French Soldier bristles from the insult.

                    FRENCH SOLDIER
          State your name and purpose.

                    JACOB
          Jacob and Wilhelm Grimm in service
          to Kassel.
                    (holds up papers)
          Official seal of Westphalia.

The doors creak open.

                    WILHELM
          When did you learn French?

                    JACOB
          Paris.

They pass through a holding tank. The Night Mare snorts at
other SCARED SOLDIERS.

          SCARED SOLDIERS   SUBTITLE
Diable cheval. Reste en   Devil horse. Stay back.
arrière.

A second set of doors open to cobblestone roads.

They clip-clop through town, passing darkened shops and
houses with seldom a light inside...

...until reaching "Wolf's Bane" Tavern Inn. Music and revelry
spill into the streets.

                    JACOB
          We're later than I intended.

                    WILHELM
          Your little firebrand holds her
          drink better than either of us.

                    JACOB
                    (dismounts)
          That's not what concerns me.

INT. BAD WILDUNGEN - TAVERN INN - NIGHT

Jacob and Wilhelm enter the two-floor establishment. A
roaring hearth takes center stage amongst the local TOWN FOLK
drinking and smoking pipes.

MUSICIANS playing a mandolin, fiddle, and flute fill the hall
with a merry tune.

At the BAR COUNTER, a walrus-mustached BARTENDER attempts to
ignore the drunken LOUSE hassling a woman covered by a RED
cloak.

20.

> LOUSE
> (slurred)
> Why not little red riding hood?
> There's beds upstairs.

> RED
> Insult me again, and we'll have a
> problem.

The Louse considers his options.

> LOUSE
> (slurred)
> Barkeep... barkeep! Give goldie
> locks another lager.

The Bartender obliges. Red swallows her beer in a single
gulp. Slams down the pewter stein.

> RED
> Thank you, now go away.

The Louse looks stupefied then angry.

> LOUSE
> You owe me!

He grabs her by the nape but she whirls, escapes from the
cloak, and kicks him in the groin -- OOOFFFF, he drops to his
knees.

MARIE, 22, athletic, long golden hair, distinct LEATHER
BRACERS, is a sight of breathtaking intensity.

She grips a sculpted ivory handle, draws her HUNTING SWORD
out and down. Stopping short of his neck.

> MARIE
> Fair warning was given.

The room's gone quiet.

KA-LACK. Marie catches sight of a FLINTLOCK PISTOL pointed at
her.

> BARTENDER
> Sheathe the blade before I put a
> hole through ya head.

Wilhelm intervenes.

> WILHELM
> Sister, there you are. We've been
> so worried.

Marie scowls as Wilhelm guides her sword back to its scabbard.

Jacob aides the Louse up onto a stool.

> BARTENDER
> *(lowers pistol)*
> You claim this woman?

> WILHELM
> Yes, fine fellow. Our mother's recent passing has left her unbalanced and prone to violence.

> BARTENDER
> Best to use a leash next time.

> WILHELM
> A proposition worth its weight in francs.

> MARIE
> *(hams it up)*
> How blessed I am for such caring brothers.

Marie swoons over Jacob and open-mouth kisses him.

The Bartender reacts with appropriate disgust.

Wilhelm slaps two Thaler coins on the bar counter and sidearm hugs the Louse.

> WILHELM
> For your trouble, and another Schwarzbier to this gentleman. No harm...
> *(sniffs the Louse)*
> ...even if considerably foul.

INT. TAVERN INN - MOMENTS LATER

The festive raucous has resumed. Jacob and Marie face each other at a table along the wall.

He scans the room for any unwanted attention as she yearns for his.

> JACOB
> You need to be more subtle.

> MARIE
> I made a valid attempt. The guy had it coming.

                    JACOB
          We all do, some sooner than others.

Marie reaches across for his hand.

                    MARIE
          But not for us.

Jacob relaxes to her touch.

                    JACOB
          I've missed you. These weeks apart
          have grown long.

She forms a giddy grin.

                    MARIE
              (softly)
          I miss feeling you between my legs.

                    JACOB
          Marie, such talk is unbecoming of a
          lady.

                    MARIE
          Who said I was a lady? You like it
          when I'm not.

Wilhelm interrupts them by setting three steins down,
splashing the beer.

                    WILHELM
          The Roggenbier is quite delicious.
              (takes a swig)
          Have you told her yet?

Marie shakes her head.

                    JACOB
          We found the Alp.

She lights up with excitement.

                    MARIE
          Remarkable!

                    WILHELM
          No, not that, I mean we did -- took
          care of it in quick fashion.

                    MARIE
          So your suspicions were correct.
          Remember to recite the adage?

                    WILHELM
          She knows?

                    MARIE
          He doesn't hold secrets from me.

                    JACOB
          At any rate, I'm pleased our
          endeavor proved successful.

                    WILHELM
          Complemented by a lemon. What
          possessed you with such insight?

                    JACOB
          Savigny's manuscripts had contained
          a fruitful passage.

                    WILHELM
          Do wonders never cease, my brother
          delivers a pun.

An ample-bosomed BARMAID serves them two plates of lung
sausage resting on a pile of mushy, chopped up cabbage.

                    WILHELM
          Mmm, Kohlwurst. Thank you...
                    (ogles the eyeful)
          ...for such a bountiful feast.

                    BARMAID
                    (smirks)
          Call upon me for anything else.

Marie glares at Wilhelm who notices as he devours his food.

                    WILHELM
          My apologies, Marie, I thought you
          had eaten.

Jacob cuts into his sausage.

                    JACOB
          Care for a taste of mine?

                    MARIE
          Always.

He blushes.

                    WILHELM
          How ever will you lovebirds survive
          another two weeks?

                    MARIE
          One exhausting night at a time.

                    WILHELM
          Why brother, have I been replaced
          on our witch hunt?

The table bumps.

                    WILHELM
          Ow!

                    MARIE
          What witch? Jacob...

At this very moment, Jacob longs to be anywhere but here. He
gulps down remainder of his liquid courage.

                    JACOB
          Tomorrow, Will and I are heading
          south towards Lichtenstein.

                    MARIE
          What about *our* hunt for the
          werewolf? You promised.

                    WILHELM
          One must learn to look beyond
          personal retributions.

                    JACOB
          There's immense evil residing in
          the Black Forest that must be
          annihilated.

                    WILHELM
          For the greater good.

Marie jerks up, rattling the table.

                    MARIE
          Greater good! Think of your father,
          my parents -- our union!

Wilhelm almost chokes on his food.

Jacob holds steady with his sympathetic expression.

                    JACOB
          I do and it will be so, but only
          after we root out *all* threats that
          veil themselves as myth.

                    MARIE
          Oh!

Overwhelmed by frustration, she storms up to the second
floor... SLAM! Jacob flinches.

                    WILHELM
          Marriage?

                    JACOB
          She has a dowry already
          established, and... I love her.

                    WILHELM
          As would have father, God rest his
          soul.

                    JACOB
          God rest his soul.

Wilhelm raises his stein.

                    WILHELM
          A toast. May her passion burn
          bright through many long years.

He polishes off his drink. Grabs the ample-bosomed Barmaid to
his knee.

                    BARMAID
               (intrigued)
          Oh!

                    WILHELM
          As for me, who am I to deny many-a-
          maiden my company?

He whisks the Barmaid about in an impromptu dance.

EXT. CASTLE WILDENBERG - NIGHT

FRIEDRICH VON SAVIGNY, 43, discerning gentleman with a pony
tail, velvet frock, strolls through a rundown arch gate and
across an expansive, unkempt lawn...

...to an imposing manor house. Sounds of a vicious dog fight
drift from the back.

INT. CASTLE WILDENBERG - STUDY

Savigny enters a room lit only by the crackling fire casting
a shadow of its sole occupant: the BARON, 74, weathered with
long scraggly hair, persistent cough, in a high-back chair.

26.

                    SAVIGNY
          Father.

                    BARON
          Such blasphemy; I have no son.

                    SAVIGNY
          I'm your only son.

Savigny faces the Baron who refuses to acknowledge him.

                    BARON
          A traitor. Smelled your stench a
          mile away.

                    SAVIGNY
          That was a lifetime ago.

                    BARON
          Your treachery continues to this
          day.

                    SAVIGNY
          Please, Father, I don't wish to
          fight. It's been so many years.

                    BARON
          Biding your time until I am weak
          and frail. Back to usurp me!

                    SAVIGNY
          Only help. They are beyond your
          reach.

The Baron shifts his intense gaze at Savigny.

                    BARON
          Not anymore.

He stands, rebuffing any help. Fixates on the large portrait
of a fetching young woman.

                    BARON
          What the elder Grimm did to your
          mother... Any whelp of that butcher
          deserves just as much.

                    SAVIGNY
          You've bloodied the water equally.
          Let this madness go before it runs
          to ruin.

The Baron lashes out, striking Savigny across the face.

                    BARON
          I am lord of this house! Abandon me
          once more, recreant, or witness the
          decimation of your wards.

INT. TAVERN INN - SECOND FLOOR HALL - LATER

Jacob loiters from door to door, lightly knocking.

                    JACOB
          Marie... Marie... Marie --

The third one swings open. Marie stands before him, robed in
her full-length red cloak.

INT. MEAGER ROOM

Inhabited by barren walls and a bed with frayed linens. Jacob
closes the door.

                    JACOB
          Are you still angry?

Marie unhooks the cloak's metal clasp. Her naked body on full
display.

                    MARIE
          Furious.

She soaks in Jacob's admiration before escaping under the bed
covers.

In a comical fashion, Jacob speed strips his many layers.

He cozies up next to Marie.

                    JACOB
          How can I make this right?

His hand explores down her body.

                    MARIE
          Take me with ah--

Her neck arches, surrendering to sensual gratification.

                    JACOB
          The dangers are unknown.

Marie stops him...

                    MARIE
          All the more reason. You'll need my
          abilities.

...disappears under the sheets. Jacob's eyes roll back as his mouth drops.

She mounts him, but Jacob turns them over to missionary.

> JACOB
> You have obligations here.

He begins a slow, rhythmic motion. They share a feeling of mutual adoration.

Marie holds Jacob close -- surprise rolls them back around.

> MARIE
> Whom a huntsman is watching over.

She sits erect, takes control.

> JACOB
> Always an answer for everything.

> MARIE
> Better you learn that now.

Jacob submits to her gyrating hips.

> JACOB
> More lessons are needed.

> MARIE
> We have time. I'm not going
> anywhere --

> JACOB
> -- without me.

Marie acknowledges her victory with a coy smile.

> MARIE
> Until death parts us.

INT. MEAGER ROOM - MORNING

Light pours in from the single window. Marie stirs, waking to find herself alone.

INT. GOTHIC CHURCH

A cavernous hall supported by stone pillars with seldom a solitary WORSHIPER occupying the otherwise vacant wooden pews.

In the front row, Jacob and Wilhelm are bent over in prayer to a suspended crucifix.

Wilhelm rises and smiles as Marie takes his place.

>   MARIE
>   You left me.

>   JACOB
>   Just so far as to absolve my sins
>   and ask forgiveness.

>   MARIE
>   Our love isn't sinful.

>   JACOB
>   Nor sanctioned.

She coos in his ear.

>   MARIE
>   A fault we can easily remedy.

EXT. BAD WILDUNGEN - GOTHIC CHURCH

Wilhelm waits on his stallion, wearing a smug grin.

>   WILHELM
>   You look fresh as the morning dew,
>   Marie. Last night proved agreeable?

Marie and Jacob both climb up on their horses.

>   MARIE
>   My affections were appeased.

>   WILHELM
>   So this isn't goodbye, but welcome.

Marie leans over to Jacob for a kiss and notices the Night
Mare's pale eyes.

>   MARIE
>   Where did you find such a unique
>   breed?

>   JACOB
>   In a dream.

MONTAGE - TRAVELING SOUTH

-- Jacob, Marie, and Wilhelm ride out of the town's gates.

-- They cross a waist-high, wide, swift flowing river.

-- Descend down a prairie hill covered by blooming wild
   flowers. The RHON MOUNTAINS rising up on the horizon.

-- Sleep under stars near a smoldering fire.

END MONTAGE

EXT. RHON MOUNTAINS - FOREST - DAY

The group navigates single file around densely populated
trees with exposed roots blanketed by moss.

                    WILHELM
          Am I mistaken, or has our direction
          veered farther east than necessary?

                    JACOB
          What was your first hint?

                    WILHELM
          The distinct regional flora.

                    MARIE
          And here I thought you only studied
          anatomy.

                    JACOB
          Marie believes the woods near
          Schwabisch Hall may hold promise.

                    WILHELM
          Hot on the trail for vengeance.

                    MARIE
          Justice. Since when does such
          distinction matter to you?

                    WILHELM
          I'm admittedly less particular.
          Savigny, on the other hand, would
          have a few words.

                    MARIE
          Again we return to him.

                    JACOB
          He is a law scholar who holds
          unusual reverence for the beast.

INT. NATIONAL LIBRARY OF FRANCE - DAY - FLASHBACK

A vast assortment of books extending up to the ceiling arches
surround a row of crowded tables.

SUPERIMPOSE: "Paris, 1805"

Near the back with only a modicum of privacy, Jacob
diligently writes as he references a propped open journal.

Savigny paces around him in a similar Parisian suit.

<table>
<tr><td>SAVIGNY</td><td>SUBTITLE</td></tr>
</table>

SAVIGNY	SUBTITLE
Terminez la dernière section et être fait pour aujourd'hui.	Finish out the last section and be done for today.

JACOB	SUBTITLE
Merci, professeur Savigny. Cela s'est avéré une découverte enrichissante.	This proved a rewarding discovery.

                    SAVIGNY
          Your French has improved at an
          excellent pace. Equal to law
          journal transcription.

Jacob sets his quill down and flips open a more delicate
manuscript.

                    JACOB
          Cultivating both allows me more
          time with the medieval texts.

                    SAVIGNY
          Do try and further this research
          when you return home.

                    JACOB
          I'll miss referencing from your
          extensive lycanthropy collection.

                    SAVIGNY
          An interest that nearly rivals my
          own.

Savigny sits opposite Jacob. He flicks past several pages
until arriving at a gruesome WEREWOLF WOODCUT.

                    SAVIGNY
          Brutal depiction from 1512. Not at
          all accurate, decapitation and
          eating of infants. Man fears what
          he doesn't understand.

                    JACOB
          Fear keeps you alive.

                    SAVIGNY
          So does prudence. No species can
          survive without it.
                    (MORE)

                    SAVIGNY (cont'd)
          Why has the werewolf legend
          flourished beyond its ancient Greek
          origin?

EXT. RHON MOUNTAINS - FOREST - DAY (1810)

                    JACOB
          "Because all great myths grow from
          a seed of truth," was his favorite
          trope.

                    MARIE
          If he only knew.

RUSTLING in the distance.

                    WILHELM
          Hold up, Jacob.

He dismounts. Brings out a LONG BARREL RIFLE from his saddle
holster.

Wilhelm positions himself under low hanging branches and
takes aim.

IN HIS SIGHTS, an 8-POINT BUCK wanders out from the brush,
grazing.

                    WILHELM (O.S.)
          There we are. Roasted venison.

The Buck raises its head -- bolts!

WILHELM frowns as he lowers the rifle.

A weary little girl in braids, GRETEL, 10, stumbles into view
and collapses.

                    WILHELM
          Jacob! Marie!

He retrieves Gretel. Gently lays her down. She's barefoot and
dirty.

                    MARIE
          The poor thing. So young to be
          wandering alone.

Jacob dribbles water from a flask to her dry, cracked lips.

                    JACOB
          The nearest village is a half-day's
          journey on foot.

Gretel coughs, sputters -- opens her eyes. She launches
herself into Marie's arms.

                    GRETEL
               (muffled dry cries)
          You found me.

Stunned, Marie holds her close while looking for guidance
from the equally bewildered brothers.

                    MARIE
          Everything's alright. Tell us what
          happened to your family.

Gretel faces her rescuers.

                    GRETEL
          Father left us in the woods to look
          for food. Now he's lost.

Jacob removes a piece of pumpernickel from his pack and hands
it to Gretel. She sniffs then consumes the bread in short
order.

                    GRETEL
          Thank you, kind sir.

                    JACOB
          Call me Jacob, and that's my
          brother Wilhelm.

                    MARIE
          I'm Marie. What's your name?

                    GRETEL
          Gretel. I escaped from an old woman
          who's a witch.

                    WILHELM
          Another one?

                    GRETEL
               (distraught)
          She has plans to eat my brother.

                    MARIE
          Jacob, we must save him.

                    GRETEL
          The witch tricked us with her house
          of sweets. Poor Hansel! Locked in a
          cage... soon the oven!

Marie comforts her while Jacob unfolds his cloth MAP.

He points out a region near the mountain range.

                    JACOB
          Here would be the most probable
          area to search, given the distance.

                    MARIE
          Where might Gretel's father have
          gone?

                    WILHELM
          Bad Brückenau isn't far off.

                    GRETEL
               (to Marie)
          Please, can we go see?

                    MARIE
          Right away.

Everyone prepares to leave.

                    JACOB
          I expect we'll rendezvous with you
          by nightfall. Should fortune favor
          us, the boy too.

Marie pulls Jacob aside for a goodbye kiss.

                    MARIE
          Safe and swift travels.

EXT. RHON MOUNTAINS - FOREST CLEARING - DUSK

A yellow-orange light filters in low, touching tops of the
forest fern bed. The brothers roam parallel to each other,
searching...

                    WILHELM
          The hour grows late and my backside
          has calloused.

                    JACOB
          Won't be much longer. Our chances
          of finding Hansel die with the
          light.

                    WILHELM
          If he even exists. Gretel could be
          a ruse of the wood nymphs. Baiting
          unsuspecting travelers on a wild
          goose chase until dead.

                    JACOB
          Should that be true, we'll add them
          to the list.

They stop in front of a small clearing unusually devoid of
any vegetation, dismount, and step onto a crushed-rock path
seven feet in length.

                    WILHELM
          If only a house was at the end of
          this path to nowhere.

Jacob surveys the area for clues.

                    JACOB
          There has to be a reason why.

                    WILHELM
          To confound us for the amusement of
          wood nymphs!

His boot kicks rock fragments that fly down the path but
disappear before landing.

Wilhelm does a double take.

                    WILHELM
          Jacob! Watch this.

He demonstrates the wonder by sliding his arm into the void.

                    JACOB
          Remarkable. What do you feel?

                    WILHELM
          Nothing.

He walks through, rapier falling off him as he vanishes.

                    JACOB
          Wilhelm!

Wilhelm reappears...

                    WILHELM
          I found it.

...pulls Jacob in.

EXT. CANDY COTTAGE - DAY

Jacob jerks back, stuck, holding a pistol crossbow that
refuses to cross over. He drops the weapon.

                    JACOB
          A clever piece of threat protection
          magic.

The gravel path winds through a well-lit arranged forest of
crooked pine trees to a cottage in the distance: all
perfectly staged like a FILM SET.

                    JACOB
          Stay alert.

They make their way along the trail.

                    WILHELM
          How difficult can an old woman be?

Small, colorful boxes filled with goodies dangle off the
branches.

                    WILHELM
          Look at all the treats. I sure am
          hungry.

                    JACOB
          Don't be foolish.

Ignoring his brother, Wilhelm reaches for a box when the
cottage door swings open.

Each leap for cover behind tree trunks less than half their
width.

A withered and feeble CRONE, 110, hobbles with a cane to a
wood pile. She picks up a log, pauses, looks directly at the
brothers.

                    CRONE
          Gretel? Gretel? Come here, child.

HER EYESIGHT shows a blurry haze of dark blotches.

JACOB watches the Crone return inside, muttering to herself.

Wilhelm smiles at him.

                    WILHELM
          Blind as a bat.

INT. CANDY COTTAGE

In a neglected condition. Rotten stench of human remains and
SPOILED CAKES in various stages of decay. Shelves are
cluttered with vials and boxes near a suspended cauldron.

                    CRONE
          Must been a bird or hare. No sign
          of your sister.

She feels for the oven door, opens, and feeds the log.

                    HANSEL (O.S.)
          How would you know?

The Crone clacks her cane against a giant IRON BIRDCAGE where
chubby, rosy-cheeked HANSEL, 12, resides.

                    CRONE
          I just do. She's gone, vanished,
          like my own -- abandoned me to
          starve. All for favor of some
          prince!

Her cane bangs the birdcage again.

                    CRONE
          Come now, boy, lets feel your
          progress.

Hansel digs around a nest of skeletal remains and sticks two
BONE FINGERS through the bars. The Crone touches them.

                    CRONE
          Three weeks and still thin!
          Wretched child, I shan't wait any
          longer.

She grabs a cake and shoves it through the cage.

                    CRONE
          Eat!

EXT. CANDY COTTAGE

Jacob observes through a window.

                    JACOB
          The boy's alive. How shall we --

He slaps Wilhelm's hand prying a gingerbread shingle with
frosting spackle.

                    WILHELM
          Ye of little faith.

Wilhelm snaps the gingerbread off and bites, relishing the
sweetness.

The Crone hustles out faster than expected.

                    CRONE
          Who's there? Who dares to eat my
          house.

Wilhelm sneaks around the other side.

                    WILHELM (O.S.)
                 (girly voice)
          It's me, Gretel. I returned from
          picking mushrooms.

                    CRONE
          Where are you, dear?

She meanders over towards Wilhelm.

INT. CANDY COTTAGE

Hansel perks up at the sight of Jacob sneaking towards him.

                    JACOB
          Gretel sends her regards.

Jacob pulls at the cage's bars.

                    HANSEL
                 (whispers)
          My sister's alive!

                    JACOB
          Safe and sound. This is quite the
          quandary you're in.

                    HANSEL
          Best hurry before the crone comes
          back.

                    JACOB
          Hand me one of those.

Hansel finds him a toothpick bone fragment. Jacob digs it
around the keyhole until SNAP!

He tries his own key to no avail.

                    JACOB
          I'm open to suggestions.

                    HANSEL
          The crone has a key.

Hansel motions around his neck, points to Jacob's.

                    HANSEL
          Hanging by a string.

                    JACOB
          As are you, I'm afraid.

                    HANSEL
          Hide!

Jacob positions himself near the shelving as the Crone enters
with Wilhelm. He shuffles on his knees, holding two more
logs.

                    CRONE
          See who's returned just in time.

                    HANSEL
          Sister, how you've changed.

The Crone rummages her shelves.

                    CRONE
          Go feed the oven's fire, child.

Wilhelm does as instructed. Leaves the oven door ajar.

                    CRONE
          Is it hot enough?

                    WILHELM
              (girly voice)
          How do you mean?

The Crone lifts a box lid -- out jumps a toad! She catches it
mid-air with lightning fast reflexes.

                    CRONE
          Ignorant dullard! The fire, feel
          its heat.

                    WILHELM
              (girly voice)
          I cannot tell.

She slams the box down --

                    CRONE
          Impossible.

-- passes by Jacob. Stops. Listens...

Inches apart, he holds his breath.

The Crone saunters on and abruptly whirls, jabbing him in the side.

                    CRONE
          Simple-minded fool!

She presses her cane against Jacob's neck.

Wilhelm leaps to his feet. He picks up a petrified braided bread and busts it over her head.

The Crone glances behind.

                    CRONE
          Útok späť.

Filthy plates with spoiled cakes levitate in unison and bombard Wilhelm.

One plate whacks his head that drops him as the rest CLATTER against a wall.

                    JACOB
          Will!

With a furious burst of strength, Jacob forces the Crone into her shelves. The contents topple off, releasing THREE TOADS.

                    JACOB
          No one hurts my brother!

They crash upon the rickety table that buckles under their weight -- flattening the first toad.

Jacob flings the cane from her grip.

                    CRONE
          Preč--

He covers her mouth. She bites his finger until it bleeds.

                    JACOB
          Aaah!

                    CRONE
          Preč s tebou!

He's thrown against the entry.

Twenty different ear-cringing sounds emit as she stands.

                    CRONE
               (to herself)
          Such insolence.
                    (MORE)

                    CRONE (cont'd)
          Enter my home, try to steal my
          food; hurt an old, fragile woman.

Sneers at Jacob.

                    CRONE
          I'll feast on your entrails!

                    WILHELM (O.S.)
          Not today.

The Crone's cane projects out from her stomach: covered in
blood and bits of tissue. She's in disbelief.

                    JACOB
          Death comes for us all, witch. We
          are yours.

He yanks the key off her neck.

                    WILHELM
          We are Death.

They shove the Crone into the oven and lock it. Agonizing
wails follow.

EXT. BLACK FOREST - CHICKEN LEG HUT - NIGHT

In the midst of a blue rose garden, Baba Yaga clutches at her
heart as if stabbed.

                    BABA YAGA
          NO! Broom ku mne!

A silver birch broom flies to her hand. She perches on the
glass mortar and takes off.

INT. CANDY COTTAGE - MOMENTS LATER

The noise has subsided. Jacob unlocks the cage, helps Hansel
out.

                    HANSEL
          Danke. She burned like tinder.

                    JACOB
          Her fire served our needs well.

                    WILHELM (O.S.)
          A-ha.

He returns from a back storage, smeared in frosting, with an
adult coat and cinched sack. Drapes the coat on Hansel.

                    JACOB
          Shouldn't that be for you?

                    WILHELM
          Only if we wish to plague ourselves
          with bad luck.

Hansel second-guesses his gift.

                    JACOB
          Ignore him. My brother's prone to
          silly superstitions.

                    WILHELM
          Silly to some.

Wilhelm opens the sack filled with coin and precious
gemstones. Selects two emeralds and hands the rest to Hansel.

                    HANSEL
          Danke! We shan't go hungry again.

                    WILHELM
          A fair day's wage.

EXT. CANDY COTTAGE - DAY

The film set facade has disintegrated. Baba Yaga soars down
from a rain cloud to the deteriorating cottage.

INT. CANDY COTTAGE

Two toads desperately squeeze under the front door -- it
opens. One leaps to the side as a boot squishes the other.

                    BABA YAGA
                 (anxious)
          Sestra? Sestra?

Dreading the inevitable, she opens the oven and crumples at
the sight of charred remains.

          BABA YAGA   SUBTITLE
Moja sestricˇka!   Baby sister!

Baba Yaga sobs but only for a moment.

          BABA YAGA   SUBTITLE
Ja sa pomstím tˇa.   I will avenge you.

Flames erupt under the tepid cauldron.

Baba Yaga tosses many vials into the water that creates a
swirling vortex of color.

She snatches the last fleeing toad and rips off its legs,
ingesting them whole...

...squeezes the toad's twitching body over the BUBBLING
CAULDRON like a tube of toothpaste until both eyes pop out --
WHOOSH! A cloud of smoke erupts.

> BABA YAGA
> Odhalit˘ môjho nepriatel˘a.

The watery reflection reveals a live broadcast of Wilhelm,
Marie, and Jacob wearing towels.

> BABA YAGA
> Destroyed by mere pups! Your folly,
> sister, won't be my own.

Baba Yaga fixates on Jacob: a crooked smile forms.

> BABA YAGA
> Yet all is not lost.

She looks to the window where a BLACK CROW waits.

> BABA YAGA
> Go my pet. Keep a watchful eye on
> our adversaries.

The crow responds with a CAW-CAW then flies off --

EXT. CANDY COTTAGE

-- squawking at the other HUNDRED CROWS that swirl up in a
tornado of feathers.

INT. SCHWÄBISCH HALL - BATH HOUSE - DAY

A sanctuary of elegant serenity.

The high domed ceiling overlooks a marble circular pool where
a dozen NUDE BATHERS of various age, size, and gender lounge.

Wilhelm eases into the warm, therapeutic bath.

> WILHELM
> Aaaah, just what my aching body
> needs. I haven't been this clean in
> a month.

> JACOB
> We're quite aware.

Marie admires Jacob's taut backside as he enters the water.
His tense muscles instantly relax.

She hesitates...

                    JACOB
          Now you're being coy?

...makes a gesture to Wilhelm.

                    MARIE
          Turn around.

                    WILHELM
          No time for modesty. What about the
          other free spirits?

                    MARIE
          Look at them.

Wilhelm averts his gaze while Jacob soaks in the visage of
Marie wading through the pool like a Greek goddess.

                    MARIE
          Very soothing but keep your
          distance, Will.

She submerges up to her neck near Jacob.

                    JACOB
          A welcomed respit before we reach
          Lichtenstein and beyond.

                    WILHELM
          There is a likelihood the Black
          Forest contains nothing of note.
          Our queen's story may just be an
          elaborate folktale created by her
          nursemaids.

                    JACOB
          Like so many others. The ideal
          outcome.

                    MARIE
          Either truth could be gleaned from
          King Frederick himself.

                    WILHELM
          Tread lightly. I've heard rumors of
          a volatile temperament.

                    MARIE
          He should at least acknowledge
          loyal servitude.

                         JACOB
               That's contingent upon being
               granted an audience.

                         WILHELM
               Or put in the stocks.

EXT. SCHWÄBISCH HALL - TOWN SQUARE - LATER

Refreshed and in a joyous mood, the three pass by a fountain -
- adorned with crows -- into a congested public market.

Among the crowd, the Baron trails them from a distance. He
pushes past others with an intimidating demeanor, keeping his
prey in sight.

                         WILHELM
               Who'd have guessed the spa could
               make one so famished?

                         JACOB
               None of your usual indulgence
               tonight.

                         MARIE
               I want to leave before dawn.

Wilhelm grumbles like a child at bedtime.

                         WILHELM
               Spoiling any chance for a proper
               feast.

EXT. SCHWÄBISCH HALL - INN

Before reaching the entrance, Marie senses something afoot
and turns around. The Baron is gone. Only fellow PATRONS.

                         JACOB
               What's wrong?

                         MARIE
               Nothing... a sudden chill came   over
               me.

Jacob wraps his arm around her.

                         JACOB
               A hearty lager shall suit us both.

EXT. BAVARIAN FOREST - MORNING

Peaceful. A rising fog hangs in the scenic landscape's upper
canopy.

                    MARIE (O.S.)
              Let's not get crass.

Three horses bearing Wilhelm, Marie, and Jacob saunter
towards a babbling brook.

                    WILHELM
              Most would consider it rather
              unseemly. No matter the reason.

The horses pause for a drink then cross it.

                    JACOB
              My safety is Marie's utmost
              importance during times of danger.

                    WILHELM
              Fearsome fat cows grazing in a
              field.

                    MARIE
              Is someone jealous? I think Jacob
              looks even more dashing.

Jacob admires the borrowed leather bracer on his arm.

                    JACOB
              Does possess a certain indefinable
              quality.

                    WILHELM
              I think the hot springs have
              muddled both your sensibilities.

                    MARIE
              Lack of animal slaughter proves
              nothing. The beast still roams free
              and mine to kill.

                    WILHELM
              Remind me to never run afoul of
              you.

SPLASH, SPLASH -- GROWL!

A scruffy GRAY WHITE WEREWOLF knocks Wilhelm off his horse.

                    MARIE
              Will!

Jacob stares wide-eyed at a FLASHBACK of his bleeding father
pinned down. Philipp reaches for him.

                          JACOB
             Father?

                       PHILIPP/MARIE
             Jacob!

JACOB snaps back to reality. Sees Wilhelm flailing his legs
at Gray White before the werewolf chomps down on one.

Wilhelm cries out.

                          MARIE
             Help him!

She lunges her sword into Gray White's side. The werewolf
howls, smacking Marie away.

Gray White pulls the sword free as Marie reaches for her
ankle sheath --

Wilhelm limps towards his rifle holster.

Marie swipes her DAGGER at Gray White in an arm's length
confrontation.

BEURRR -- a bolt penetrates the werewolf's back.

Gray White mauls Jacob to the ground -- pistol-crossbow falls
from reach -- he lodges his bracer against ravenous jaws.

Marie slashes madly from behind, creating red gashes among
the matted fur until --

The werewolf lacerates her exposed arm. Intense pain causes
Marie to withdraw into a defensive fetal position.

KA-BOOM! A branch splinters above them.

Wilhelm begins reloading, sees the werewolf charge.

Gray White strikes; Wilhelm dodges, pulls his flintlock
pistol --

A claw swats it from his hand.

Wilhelm counters with a rifle butt to Gray White's jaw, flips
it around: KA-BOOM! Point-blank shot into the stomach.

From the brush, a stronger SILVERBACK WEREWOLF ambushes
Wilhelm.

                          JACOB
             No!

Jacob levels his full-size crossbow. Expertly fires TWO BOLTS at the same time --

-- one grazes Silverback's neck and the other punctures a pectoral muscle.

Jacob smashes the crossbow across Silverback's face, dropping the werewolf.

He casts the crossbow aside, scoops up Marie's sword.

                    JACOB
          DIE BEAST!

Raises the weapon and halts.

                    JACOB
          Impossible.

Laying beneath him is an injured Savigny.

Mouth agape, he falters back, sword slipping from his grip.

                    WILHELM (O.S.)
          Jacob, I'm safe... look!

Jacob acknowledges his brother with bewilderment.

                    WILHELM
          No harm came to me.

Marie retrieves her ivory handle and approaches the hemorrhaging Baron.

His sunken face glowers at her as blood seeps from the gaping wound.

She observes his suffering with more pity than hatred. Positions her sword over him...

                    MARIE
          May we both find peace.

...and impales his chest.

EXT. BAVARIAN FOREST - LATER

Bandaged as needed, everyone huddles around a small fire. A heavy silence hangs in the air.

Savigny is covered by a blanket and donated trousers. He gauges the introspective mood.

                    SAVIGNY
          I'm grateful to see no serious harm
          came upon you. If only I'd been
          more adept at tracking his
          whereabouts.

                    JACOB
          All these years and you never told
          me.

                    SAVIGNY
          This damnation spans generations.
          It's a secret not easily broached.
          Mentoring you was my only means for
          atonement. I couldn't risk
          rejection or worst.

                    WILHELM
          You knew what happened.

                    SAVIGNY
          My brother's aggression was an
          unfortunate tragedy.

                    JACOB
               (realizing)
          When he attacked us as children.

                    SAVIGNY
          No doubt, at the bidding of our
          father. The outcome only served to
          enrage him.

                    MARIE
          My parents died by his savagery!

                    SAVIGNY
          I am truly sorry. No words can
          amend years of reckless bloodlust.
               (to Jacob)
          A consequence of protecting you
          boys from reprisal.

                    JACOB
          What grievance could justify such a
          cycle of bitterness?

                    SAVIGNY
          That pebble shall remain forever
          lost among the rubble.

                    WILHELM
          Then I say it's time we close this
          chapter and set forth anew.

                    SAVIGNY
          Allow me to bury my father and any
          further discord between us.

Marie chooses her words carefully.

                    MARIE
          Retribution's been served. Please
          accept my horse as goodwill.

Savigny reaches out to her.

                    SAVIGNY
          Generosity beyond compare. One day
          we'll meet under more hospitable
          circumstances.

                    JACOB
          At our wedding.

Marie tackles Jacob with a joyous hug.

                    MARIE
          Yes, you must attend.

                    SAVIGNY
          I'd be honored. When's the affair?

                    MARIE
          We haven't discussed.

                    JACOB
          Soon. Upon our return to Kassel.

EXT. LICHTENSTEIN VILLAGE - DAY

In shambles. Marie rides with Jacob on the Night Mare,
passing buildings damaged or destroyed...

...stopping in front of "Sphinx's Riddle" tavern. A crow
lands on the dangling sign and caws as they enter.

INT. SPHINX'S RIDDLE

Greeted by a sculpted wooden sphinx and empty dining area.

                    WILHELM
          Find more action in a graveyard.

                    MARIE
          We do get our pick of the tables.

Jacob trails after Marie.

Wilhelm parks himself at the BAR COUNTER next to a blubbering
spineless tailor, DEDRICK, 33, short and balding with a
rumpled suit, drowning his sorrows in a lager.

A thick, female MANNISH BARKEEP, 40s, greets her new customer
with a blank stare while scrubbing a stein.

                    WILHELM
          Excuse me.

She sets the stein down, picks up a new one.

                    WILHELM
          I wish to speak with the
          proprietor.

                    MANNISH BARKEEP
          You are.

                    WILHELM
          Oh, how progressive. My friends and
          I are in need of a good meal.

                    MANNISH BARKEEP
          Must be new in town.

                    WILHELM
          We've traveled a considerable
          distance.

                    MANNISH BARKEEP
          Shelves are bare. Tapped my last
          barrel of Doppelbock.

                    WILHELM
          Sold! Has the town experienced a
          recent disaster?

She fills three STEINS until each holds a frothy head above
the rim.

                    MANNISH BARKEEP
          Often.

Wilhelm pays her a little extra and gestures at Dedrick.

                    WILHELM
          What's his story?

                    MANNISH BARKEEP
          Enjoy the beer. Get back to
          wherever that might be before its
          too late.

She collects his coins and returns to cleaning. Wilhelm
clinks the steins together as he gathers them.

He joins Jacob and Marie at their table. Distributes the
drinks.

                    WILHELM
          The owner wasn't very helpful.

More bawling from the bar.

                    MARIE
          Neither is that noise.

Marie kicks her chair back, and sidles up to DEDRICK who
gives her the once-over.

                    MARIE
          Pardon my intrusion. Can I offer
          any relief from your troubles?

                    DEDRICK
          I've no coin to tender but would
          appreciate the company. It shall be
          my last time.

He bursts into tears again.

                    MARIE
          Why you little worm.

Jacob intervenes.

                    JACOB
          Think of such comments as a
          compliment.

                    JACOB
               (to Dedrick)
          We can assist in other ways. Please
          join us.

AT THE TABLE, Wilhelm welcomes Dedrick to an open chair.
Dedrick immediately polishes off his own drink and proceeds
to guzzle Jacob's.

                    DEDRICK
          Thank you for this kindness.
          Dedrick's my name, the village
          tailor.

                    WILHELM
          A man who aspires beyond his
          station.

                    DEDRICK
          A father's wishful thinking. Who
          are you folk?

                    JACOB
          Historical linguists from
          Westphalia --

                    WILHELM
          Yoke of the French.

                    JACOB
          -- sent by Queen Catharina.

                    DEDRICK
          Here? Are you being punished?

                    MARIE
          What has stricken you with such
          grief?

                    DEDRICK
          I've been ordered to seek help from
          Baba Yaga, a witch who lives in the
          Black Forest.

                    WILHELM
          Perfect!

His enthusiasm quickly softens in light of Dedrick's
pronounced distress.

                    MARIE
          Wouldn't the king's guard be better
          suited?

Dedrick lays out a belt with the words "Seven at one blow"
stitched across.

                    DEDRICK
          My boasting of dead flies reached
          King Frederick as a tale of bravery
          against seven large ruffians. He
          promised riches and land upon
          completion.

                    WILHELM
          Your name proved to be prophetic.

                    DEDRICK
          Only if I live.

                    JACOB
          Allow us to accompany your quest
          nevertheless.

                    DEDRICK
          More lambs to slaughter. What can a
          linguist do about giants?

                         MARIE
          Giants!

                    JACOB
          We possess other skills.

EXT. BLACK FOREST - DAY - FLASHBACK (1788)

Blood-curdling SHRIEKS scatter woodland creatures just before
branches break from the Chicken Leg Hut CLUMPING past.

                    DEDRICK (V.O.)
          Some believe B-b-baba Yaga holds
          dominion over the giants. Sends
          them at her leisure.

The shrieking echos throughout HELL'S VALLEY. Drifts down a
winding mountain path, fades... then the ground shakes, rocks
tumble, an earthquake!

EXT. CASTLE LICHTENSTEIN - DAY

Majestic white stone. Barely discernible in thick fog from
the cliff it's built on.

Two GIANTS emerge, frightening behemoths forty-feet tall,
climbing up the side.

MAGOG, lanky and cunning, scales the wall first. Bashes a
tower with his CLUB.

Several Royal Guards jab at him with pikes.

Magog snatches a guard, breaks his neck, and hangs him on a
belt hook like a trophy.

SIGENOT, bald with a bristly beard, all muscle no brain,
reaches through a carriage house roof.

He tosses a distraught peasant over his shoulder and ingests
a goat.

END FLASHBACK

55.

EXT. BLACK FOREST - WATERFALL - DAY (1810)

Dedrick guides Jacob, Marie, and Wilhelm through dense
vegetation on horseback.

                    DEDRICK
          Plagued our lands ever since.

                    JACOB
          How often do these raids occur?

                    DEDRICK
          Can't say. Does a criminal tally
          his lashings?

Sounds of rushing water. Dedrick reaches open land first; his
horse rears up --

Dumping him to the edge of a 1500-foot SHEER DROP. He peers
over, yelps, and backs away.

                    MARIE
          What a magnificent view.

Wilhelm focuses on a pile of jagged rocks that greet the
waterfall.

                    WILHELM
          Lucky fellow.

Jacob extends his hand to Dedrick who's frozen in place but
has an uncontrollable stammer.

                    DEDRICK
          I made an error. We rode too far
          south. The old hag lies northwest.

                    MARIE
          From where the river flows.

A mob of crows passes overhead, squawking in unison. They
circle several times like vultures then continue on.

                    WILHELM
          Follow the harbingers of doom.

                    DEDRICK
          Unnatural behavior.

                    JACOB
          Suspicious, at the very least. Keep
          your wits about you. Satan himself
          may be waiting for us.

EXT. BLACK FOREST - CHICKEN LEG HUT - DAY

The group reaches the small clearing that shows no evidence of the queen's story. Baba Yaga appears in her seductive MISTRESS guise.

> WILHELM
> (murmurs)
> What breed of "old hag" is she?

Baba Yaga greets them with a wave and cordial smile.

They dismount. Jacob yanks the trembling Dedrick along.

> BABA YAGA
> Welcome, expected guests.

Crows are nestled all across the mossy roof. One swoops down and lands on her shoulder.

> JACOB
> Friends of yours?

She pets the crow before it flies off.

> BABA YAGA
> They keep me company. Are you here
> by compulsion or free will?

> JACOB
> Both.

Baba Yaga slinks over to Jacob.

> BABA YAGA
> Dual purpose then. Let he who
> represents the rancorous ruler
> speak first.

She circles around the group, sizing up Marie in the process...

> DEDRICK
> (stutters)
> The king humbly asks for your help
> with the giants.

> BABA YAGA
> Giants are a ferocious lot. I've
> crossed paths with them in more...
> troubling times.

...lingers in front of an enamored Wilhelm who laps up her flirtatious teasing.

                    BABA YAGA
          You seek a potion bestowing
          permanent slumber but requires a
          rare ingredient: mandrake root.

                    WILHELM
          Whatever is needed m'lady. We can
          retrieve any and everything.

                    BABA YAGA
          I know of only one location for
          mandrake root. It grows in the
          Falkenstein ruins.

                    DEDRICK
          Falkenstein ruins lie above Hell's
          Valley.

                    JACOB
          Where these giants supposedly
          exist.

                    BABA YAGA
          Best hurry. The mountain pass is
          treacherous in light and deadly at
          night.

                    MARIE
          There's no time to lose.

She pushes the brothers toward a hasty exit when Baba Yaga
grabs Marie's wrist.

                    BABA YAGA
          Please stay. Rarely do I receive
          visitors.

Marie looks to Jacob who nods.

                    MARIE
          I accept your gracious offer.

                    BABA YAGA
          We'll share in stories and tea.

EXT. HELL'S VALLEY - DUSK

Jacob keeps careful watch as he leads on the Night Mare.

Dedrick travels between the brothers, flinching at every
noise along the way. He points out --

> DEDRICK
> Up there. The r-r-ruins rest on
> that mountain ledge.

-- the remnants of a dilapidated stronghold set upon a high
outcropping.

> JACOB
> Looks like a steep climb. Best we
> continue on foot.

> WILHELM
> Maybe ask a giant to lift us?

THUD, THUD. The ground vibrates under them.

> DEDRICK
> HIDE!

He hightails it to a nearby cave.

INT. CAVE

Jacob and Wilhelm discover Dedrick cowering in a corner.

> WILHELM
> Easy now, I was only joking.

The tailor's whole body trembles.

> DEDRICK
> Q-q-quiet.

THUD, THUD -- MOOOOOOO! Dedrick covers his ears.

Everyone waits on bated breath.

SNIFF. A gust of air exits the cave. SNIFFFFF! Jacob and
Wilhelm brace themselves from the monstrous suction.

> SIGENOT (O.S.)
> Food.

MOOOOOO! An ENORMOUS HAND lodges itself in the opening.

Wilhelm stares flabbergasted at Jacob.

The hand breaks free.

> SIGENOT (O.S.)
> Hungry.

MOOOO -- CRUNCH... SPLAT! The cave shakes as Sigenot
continues walking until no longer felt.

Jacob gathers his crossbow, satchel, and a lantern.

                    JACOB
          Shall we?

EXT. HELL'S VALLEY

The three give wide berth to the remains of a half-eaten cow.
Dedrick gags, covers his mouth.

                    WILHELM
          Do you wager it was a snack or
          dinner?

                    DEDRICK
          Let's be quick before the answer is
          known.

                    WILHELM
          And return to that beautiful
          creature.

                    JACOB
          A witch, don't forget, alone with
          Marie.

                    DEDRICK
          Should you have left her?

                    JACOB
          We had little choice. Couldn't risk
          sealing your fate to giants.

                    WILHELM
          Besides, Marie's more than capable
          of protecting herself.

                    JACOB
          I hope so.

EXT. BLACK FOREST - CHICKEN LEG HUT - SAME

Marie accepts a cup of hot tea from Baba Yaga.

                    MARIE
          Thank you.

She sips, surprised by the pleasant taste.

                    MARIE
          Mmm. Delicious.

                    BABA YAGA
          An old family recipe.

                    MARIE
          I must confess, you're not at all
          how the tailor described.

                    BABA YAGA
          Simple minds will believe any
          falsehood. I'm nothing more than a
          soothsayer, purveyor of knowledge.
          Persecuted for the weaknesses of
          royalty.

                    MARIE
          You were *familiar* with King
          Frederick?

                    BABA YAGA
          Long ago before his title. Similar
          to what you share with Jacob. I can
          tell he's a fine man.

                    MARIE
          None better.

Baba Yaga plucks a blue rose and hands it to Marie.

                    BABA YAGA
          A shame love is often like this
          rose. Beautiful to behold, but will
          soon wither and die.

                    MARIE
               (upset)
          I'm not sure I understand.

                    BABA YAGA
          Your time with Jacob has reached
          its end.

                    MARIE
          No. You lie.

Marie throws down the rose and draws her sword.

                    BABA YAGA
          Hard truths cut the deepest. Once
          Jacob falls under my spell -- as
          all men do -- he shall fulfill the
          need Frederick failed on.
               (evil grin)
          Perpetuate my line by his seed.

                    MARIE
          Never! You'll never have him!

She attacks --

Four DISEMBODIED HANDS suddenly appear and restrain her,
seizing the sword.

                    BABA YAGA
          It's a rare treat for someone to
          surprise me.

Baba Yaga runs her fingers through a lock of Marie's hair.

                    BABA YAGA
          My tea always cripples the wayward
          traveler, yet here you stand. A
          mystery I shall relish in solving.

She walks away: beauty veneer melting off with each step.

The ground rumbles underneath Marie...

                    MARIE
          What?

...and erupts into a geyser of earth, blasting her up like an
express elevator!

She jerks to a stop. Watches as the dirt encapsulates around
her into a room with a small window.

The TOWER OF SOD solidifies sixty-feet high. Thorny vines
wrap all the way to the top that has no apparent opening.

EXT. FALKENSTEIN RUINS - NIGHT

Jacob, Wilhelm, and Dedrick traipse through the desolate
structure. Jacob holds his lantern; Wilhelm a torch.

                    DEDRICK
          I've heard the ruins are cursed.

                    JACOB
          Unlikely. In our experience, curses
          rarely amount to any consequence.

                    WILHELM
          The same can also be said of magic
          beans.

They pass under the last standing archway and navigate down
crumbling stairs.

EXT. FALKENSTEIN RUINS - GRAVEYARD

Nestled in the back with a single tree.

                    JACOB
          Over there.

He leads them past weathered headstones to a patch of
Mandrake: a broad-leaf purple flower growing under three
dangling skeletons.

                    DEDRICK
          Dead man's row.

                    WILHELM
          They're all dead here.

Wilhelm plants the torch. Jacob fishes out a roll of burlap
twine.

                    JACOB
          Should have brought a dog.

                    WILHELM
          Not to worry.

He distributes rudimentary ear plugs.

                    WILHELM
          Made these myself. Put the wool
          side in your ears. The pitch should
          muffle the noise -- just keep your
          distance from fire.

                    DEDRICK
          Noise from what?

Jacob throws the twine over a branch and ties it to a
Mandrake plant.

                    JACOB
          Pay close attention.

He wraps the twine around his hands.

                    JACOB
          The soil is soft. Ready?

Wilhelm flashes his rapier in the moonlight.

Jacob tugs the twine down.

Up pops a screaming MANDRAKE ROOT! Wilhelm slices through its
"face."

                    WILHELM
          Disgusting genus.

ROTTING HANDS break through near the headstones.

Jacob places the mandrake root in his satchel. Notices the tailor passed out nearby.

                    JACOB
          Dedrick?

Wilhelm holds the lantern close to Dedrick's ear.

                    WILHELM
          No blood. Perhaps he fainted.

He lightly taps Dedrick who startles awake, disoriented.

                    JACOB
          Better than the alternative.

DECAYING BODIES emerge from the ground.

                    WILHELM
          You missed all the fun. Time to go,
          we've lingered here --

                    JACOB
          Too long!

Rising before them is a HORDE OF UNDEAD! The mob of decomposition plods forward.

                    DEDRICK
          D-d-d-d-d-

Dedrick faints again.

                    JACOB
          Why'd we bring him?

He surveys the danger with a look reminiscent of his father.

The Undead encroach from all angles.

Wilhelm's poised for action, becoming anxious.

                    WILHELM
          Our exit's blocked. What do we do?

Jacob fires a bolt that shatters exposed skull.

                    JACOB
          Stay alive.

A bony hand grabs Dedrick's foot. Wilhelm cleaves it off at the elbow. Drags the tailor farther back.

Jacob shoots a second bolt just as an unnoticed corpse
pounces --

                    WILHELM
          Jacob!

His rapier severs the Undead's stomach -- body dropping as
two pieces.

                    JACOB
               Thanks.

But its torso springs back to life and scrambles up Jacob's
back.

                    JACOB
          Augh!

Chomps down on --

A bolt. Jammed in. Putrid mouth unable to shut.

Jacob throws off the corpse. Crushes its head under his boot.

New threats converge on Wilhelm. BAM! Hits one in the
shoulder that twirls like a ballerina.

He slashes wildly at anything that gets close -- stops a
hair's breadth from Jacob's face.

They share a morbid moment.

A plump and portly corpse interrupts.

Jacob shoves the torch inside its swollen belly, instantly
lighting the zombified-tallow.

Blazing like a bonfire, the life-size candle sets other
Undead on fire as it aimlessly lumbers about.

                    JACOB
               He should burn long after we're
               gone.

                    WILHELM
               Which better be soon...

He tosses a pistol to Jacob who presses the barrel against
slimy face flesh: BAM! Two corpses topple.

                    WILHELM
               ...no more powder.

Overrun by Undead, the brothers drag Dedrick to the
graveyard's drop-off.

Jacob holds his lantern over the side. Black emptiness.

                    JACOB
          Our only avenue for escape.

                    WILHELM
          Where? I see nothing.

                    JACOB
          There's no other way.

He props up and slaps Dedrick's face.

                    JACOB
               Wake up!

Jacob throws his lantern down, sets the grass ablaze.

                    WILHELM
               Jump!

They plummet into the dark abyss...

...land and tumble for twenty feet, stopping on a jutted out
boulder. Aching groans follow.

The boulder loosens and breaks free --

                    JACOB
               Off, off!

They scoot just as it rolls down, inducing a tumultuous rock
slide that echos throughout.

                    WILHELM
          Too close for my comfort.

Like an aftershock, the mountainside shudders underfoot.

                    SIGENOT (O.S.)
               Rock hit Sigenot!

EXT. HELL'S VALLEY - NIGHT

Three figures flee under the moon's light -- thudding sounds
behind them.

                    DEDRICK
                 (stutters)
               Go faster!

Wilhelm suddenly stumbles. Jacob doubles back and lifts him.

> WILHELM
> Heart... I can't...

Jacob checks over his shoulder. A bearded monstrosity advances closer.

> JACOB
> I'm my brother's keeper. Just a
> little further.

He assists Wilhelm past the fly-buzzing cow corpse.

INT. CAVE

Their horses seem apathetic to the impending danger.

> WILHELM
> Hooray for animals loyal beyond
> sense.

Without hesitation, Dedrick gallops off.

> JACOB
> Wait!

> WILHELM
> Curse the fool who has none.

EXT. HELL'S VALLEY - CAVE

The brothers dash out just as a MAMMOTH TREE crashes down.

They race along the valley floor.

WHOOSH! WHOOSH! A constant dodge and swerve of Sigenot's
swatting tree.

> SIGENOT
> Stay still.

Another miss smashes the tree against a rock face, producing
a shower of leaves.

> JACOB
> Make for the hidden passage!

They round a bend towards a narrow ravine in the mountainside
where a creek empties out.

> SIGENOT
> Little mites move fast.

The giant leaps in front and blocks their escape. The Night
Mare rears up, dumping Jacob before --

Sigenot scoops up the horse in one hand, Dedrick in another.
All wailing in terror.

>   SIGENOT
>   Yum, yum.

Jacob watches in wonder as the Night Mare dissolves into
PIXIE DUST like a fading firework between Sigenot's teeth.

The giant reacts befuddled.

>   DEDRICK
>   Hellllp! D-d-don't eat me!

Pokes at his other "food" to verify solidity.

>   SIGENOT
>   Quiet.

>   DEDRICK
>   Hellll--

SQUISH! Giant fingers flatten Dedrick's head.

Jacob winces. Wilhelm rides over and hoists him up.

>   WILHELM
>   No helping the poor fellow now.

They speed under the giant, losing sight of Dedrick as
Sigenot chomps down.

EXT. BLACK FOREST - CHICKEN LEG HUT - NIGHT

The weary brothers arrive to find no one. An eerie silence
permeates the surrounding forest.

>   JACOB
>   Marie?

>   WILHELM
>   (calls out)
>   Baba Yaga.

INT. SOD TOWER

Marie sees them from her window.

>   MARIE
>   Jacob, up here! I'm up here!

She leans out and hits her head on the open space.

                    MARIE
          Ow.

Presses against the barrier akin to invisible plexiglass.

                    MARIE
               (pounds her fists)
          No, no, no! Stop!

Starts digging her dagger into the soil wall but any damage
magically repairs itself.

OUTSIDE, Marie's muffled cries go unheard.

                    BABA YAGA (O.S.)
          We've been anxiously awaiting you.

Wilhelm and Jacob wander past the solid sod tower...

                    WILHELM
          Don't recall that being there.

...and step inside the hut as its mouth-door closes behind
them.

The wall of posts rises up, decorated by skulls.

INT. CHICKEN LEG HUT

A destitute space comprised of little beyond a boiling
cauldron and straw bed.

Baba Yaga looks her most enticing yet in a plunging neckline,
double-slit dress: the Venus flytrap for men.

Wilhelm becomes weak in the knees. Holds out the root.

                    WILHELM
          I have --

                    JACOB
          Where's Marie?

                    BABA YAGA
          Three departed, only two return.

She plays full-court press with her feminine wiles.

                    BABA YAGA
          What ever happened to the brave
          little tailor?

                    WILHELM
          He lost his head.

                    BABA YAGA
          Pity. I'm so pleased you were
          triumphant. Giants can be most
          unpleasant.

Wilhelm welcomes her soft touch across his cheek.

                    BABA YAGA
          Stick your root in my pot.

He does as instructed. The bubbling liquid simmers to a
calming blue elixir.

                    JACOB
          Where - is - Marie.

                    BABA YAGA
          She's gone. My admission of our
          future copulation drove her away.

                    JACOB
          Deceitful temptress, you confuse
          reality with fantasy.

                    BABA YAGA
          They exist one in the same.

                    JACOB
          Tell me now!

                    BABA YAGA
          A reward first.

Baba Yaga plants her luscious lips on Wilhelm's that causes
instant metamorphosis.

A TOAD drops in the pile of his former clothing.

                    JACOB
          WILHELM!

Jacob reaches for the rapier -- three pairs of disembodied
hands subdue him.

                    JACOB
          No, stop! Reverse the spell!

Baba Yaga dips a goblet in the cauldron while musing over his
effort to break free.

                    BABA YAGA
            Why do you struggle?

She holds the goblet up to him.

                    BABA YAGA
            Drink. Free yourself of pointless
            burdens.

Jacob strains to avoid, keeping his lips sealed.

                    BABA YAGA
            Let us bed and save my clan from
            extinction. Nothing is more noble
            of an endeavor.

                    JACOB
            I rather burn you to ash.

                    BABA YAGA
            A sentiment shared by many.

Two of the disembodied hands force his jaw open. She pours in
a considerable amount.

                    BABA YAGA
            Hard truths cut the deepest.

The elixir works fast: Jacob enters a dreamy, drunken state.

Baba Yaga guides him to the straw bed.

                    BABA YAGA
            And I always speak the truth.

She stands over him, disrobes.

INT. SOD TOWER

Marie falls back, depleted, tears sliding down. Not a single
blemish on the dirt cell.

She traces over teeth marks on her bracer.

                    MARIE
            Jacob...

INT. MEAGER ROOM - NIGHT - FLASHBACK

Marie and Jacob lay in bed post-coitus. He nibbles up her arm
to neck. She squirms, giggles.

                    MARIE
            Stop.

                    JACOB
          I can't. Such sumptuous beauty.

Marie holds him back.

                    MARIE
          Will your brother be cross about
          tomorrow?

                    JACOB
          He holds you in high regard --
          thought father would approve.

                    MARIE
          Ah, yes. The wellspring of all male
          Grimm charm.

                    JACOB
          My mother did bear nine children.

More giggles.

                    MARIE
          Mine wasn't nearly so bold,
          practical yet held to old beliefs.
          She bestowed her blessing on me
          shortly before...

Marie can't bring herself to speak the tragedy.

                    JACOB
          A mother's blessing is more than
          mere whimsy.

                    MARIE
          A cherished memory.

                    JACOB
          True, but also her final gift.
          Spiritual protection that resides
          within.

INT. SOD TOWER - NIGHT

Filtered moonlight shines on the dagger laying nearby. In a
melancholy trance, Marie picks it up.

                    MARIE
          A gift within.

She teases her finger over the blade tip until breaking skin.
An unnoticed BLOOD DROP lands on the dirt floor.

The tower tremors, jolting Marie from her stupor.

She reflects on her bleeding. Squeezes out a second drop.

More tremors. A burst of inspiration!

Marie places the blade inside her hand and slices it open.
Spatters blood across the wall.

EXT. SOD TOWER

All thorny vines spontaneously wilt before the tower loses
stability and collapses on itself.

Marie breaks through the dirt mound, coughing and wheezing.

INT. CHICKEN LEG HUT

A blurry, spinning image of Baba Yaga comes into focus on her
true HIDEOUS HAG appearance.

> JACOB
> Who, who are you? Where am I?

The witch bares her rotten teeth in a gruesome grin.

Long, calcified nails pat her belly.

> BABA YAGA
> I'm the vessel of your seed.

> JACOB
> Impossible.

He becomes nauseated then vomits.

> BABA YAGA
> Recompense for killing my sister.
> Along with your quickening
> mortality.

Jacob staggers to his feet, grasping a flintlock pistol.

> BABA YAGA
> As clarity fades, death ensues: a
> necessary cycle. All vices hold a
> price, and mandrake's no different.

His aim wavers as he cocks the hammer.

> JACOB
> G-give... give me Will.

Baba Yaga feels no threat.

                    BABA YAGA
          No.

BAM! She waves the lead ball away, causing a wide miss.

                    BABA YAGA
          Your brother shall provide suitable
          nourishment to my womb.

Jacob reels around, picks up the rapier, and stabs the mouth-
door -- it screeches open. He lurches forward.

                    BABA YAGA
          Shut your mouth!

EXT. BLACK FOREST - CHICKEN LEG HUT

Jacob topples off as the hut rises.

OOOFF! Lands in front of its grotesque chicken legs just
before they hurdle the wall.

Chicken Leg Hut disappears from view, shrieking.

Marie scrambles over to him.

                    MARIE
          Jacob!

He's clammy, pale, delirious; death warmed over.

                    MARIE
          Say something. Where's Will?

She searches for signs of life.

                    MARIE
          Jacob?

No response.

Marie drags Jacob to the stallion...

                    MARIE
          I - forbid - you - to die.

...hoists him across with every last bit of strength.

Then wipes her bloody hand over three posts. Instant
retraction!

Marie pulls herself up behind Jacob.

>   MARIE
>   Stay with me.

She cracks the reins.

EXT. CASTLE LICHTENSTEIN - COURTYARD - MORNING

The gate opens to a stallion bearing two riders slumped over.

>   MARIE
>   Help.

Exhausted beyond reason, she slides off.

INT. CASTLE LICHTENSTEIN - BED CHAMBER - LATER

Jacob wakes to find himself in a luxurious bed under the
watchful eye of Marie.

>   JACOB
>   Beautiful Weisse Frau, am I dead?

He touches Marie's cheek.

>   MARIE
>   (tears up)
>   Not today.

She kisses and holds his hand close with her uninjured one.

>   JACOB
>   I'm so grateful it's you.

>   MARIE
>   What happened with Baba Yaga?

>   JACOB
>   She drugged me with her mandrake
>   potion. Everything after...

>   MARIE
>   You're safe now, nothing else
>   matters. These past two days have
>   brought little relief.

>   JACOB
>   Two days?

>   MARIE
>   The king's physician was not
>   confident.

>   JACOB
>   Oh no, Wilhelm!

INT. CASTLE LICHTENSTEIN - THRONE ROOM - DAY

Jacob and Marie stand in a cavernous hall of columns and chandeliers before the forlorn KING FREDERICK, 56, brooding from a raised platform.

His royal garments mirror the younger portrait behind him though are considerably more stretched.

                    FREDERICK
          Out of the question! I've risked
          enough granting you refuge.

                    JACOB
          Your highness, please reconsider,
          time is of the essence. My brother
          remains in danger.

                    FREDERICK
          If not already eaten. It's clear to
          me now, the tailor was sent on a
          fool's errand.

                    JACOB
          I won't give up on him!

Frederick slams his fist down.

                    FREDERICK
          Then leave! Meet the fate of my
          kingdom at a quicker pace.

Jacob's defiance shrinks into defeat.

Marie steps forward, ignoring Frederick's creepy leer.

                    MARIE
          What if we were to kill the giants?

The king responds with uproarious laughter.

                    FREDERICK
          By all means, vanquish our foes.
          I'll grant a hundred horsemen to
          storm the witch's keep and half of
          my kingdom as reward.

EXT. CASTLE LICHTENSTEIN - REMOTE WATCH TOWER

Marie consoles Jacob at a stone wall overlooking the chasm below.

76.

                    JACOB
          I was suppose to be his protector
          and failed.

                    MARIE
          Take heart, Wilhelm's the
          resourceful sort. We can still
          rescue him.

                    JACOB
          But to gain the king's favor...

Marie redirects his attention.

                    MARIE
          Put little value in empty promises.
          You shall find a way.

Jacob gazes into her eyes... then past at an ETHEREAL WOMAN
perched on the edge. Brushing her hair in the sunlight as the
rays appear to pass through her body.

                    JACOB
          Look.

Marie turns just as Ethereal Woman skips along the wall and
disappears.

They scurry after, catching sight of her at the tower door.

She pays them a glance then passes through it.

INT. WATCH TOWER

An open space containing a weapons rack and staircase along
the wall.

                    MARIE
          Now where?

A TOWER GUARD descends from the upper deck.

                    TOWER GUARD
          This area is off limits.

                    MARIE
          We are honored guests of the king.

She moseys over to the weapons.

                    JACOB
          Granted access throughout the
          castle grounds.

                    TOWER GUARD
          No one but the guard --

THWACK! Marie knocks him out cold with a pike.

                    JACOB
          Effectively blunt tactic.

Jacob pulls up a trap door. Smirks.

                    JACOB
          I'm glad you never learned
          otherwise.

INT. WATCH TOWER - CELLAR

A faint glow shimmers off the stone wall as Jacob and Marie
round the stairwell holding a torch.

                    MARIE
          I've no desire to witness horrors
          of the tower dungeon.

They enter a musty room. He casts light over crates and
crates of foodstuff.

                    JACOB
          No torture, only provisions. Hidden
          from marauding giants.

Marie wanders over to an adjoining alcove.

INT. WATCH TOWER - CHAPEL

Cobwebs adorn a stone altar where a small wooden cross stands
beneath narrow stained-glass windows.

                    MARIE
          Near a forsaken sanctuary.

                    JACOB
          Most castle defenses believed the
          best protection was a godly one.

                    MARIE
          A sentiment that's been lost here.

Jacob houses the torch in a nearby sconce.

                    JACOB
          I feel like we should.

They kneel on the bare slab and bow in prayer.

                         JACOB
          O Lord, grant us hope in times of
          despair. Please shield Wilhelm from
          unfriendly eyes. Bless and keep him
          safe. Thank you, God, for Marie.

Marie cracks a smile.

                         JACOB
          For her love and strength when I
          needed it most. Fill me with
          resolve, O Lord. Show us the way.
          In Jesus' name.

                         JACOB/MARIE
          Amen.

Marie touches his shoulder.

                         MARIE
          He isn't lost from us yet.

They proceed out when a BRILLIANT LIGHT emerges.

Both stop, shield their eyes.

The Ethereal Woman illuminates in front of the altar.

                         JACOB
          Are you a ghost?

                         ETHEREAL WOMAN
          A guardian.

Her voice is haunting and calm.

                         JACOB
          I don't understand.

                         ETHEREAL WOMAN
          Only those who prove worthy may
          entreat my favor.

                         JACOB
          Why manifest in our presence?

                         ETHEREAL WOMAN
          On account of what was entrusted by
          another.

She fades away. In her place is a 17th century STRONGBOX
equipped with handles on either side.

Jacob removes his key, suddenly feeling hesitant and apprehensive. Marie offers silent reassurance.

The key inserts perfectly and triggers the grinding sound of a metallic release.

He lifts up the lid.

                    MARIE
          Empty?

Jacob pats the box down until touching "air" that feels like cloth. Pulls out an INVISIBLE CLOAK and disappears upon robing himself.

                    JACOB (O.S.)
          Remarkable.

Marie picks up a leather-bound book stamped by a GRIMM INSIGNIA. Opens to the inside cover with a handwritten passage.

She passes it to Jacob.

                    JACOB
          To my sons. Learn from the past,
          don't be burdened by it...

EXT. WESTERN FOREST - DAY - FLASHBACK

A young PHILIPP, 20s, roasts game on a spit. Around him are several boulders and a large tree stump.

                    PHILIPP (V.O.)
          Know above all, the seeds of my
          death were sowed years before your
          birth -- by accident.

                    TROLL VOICE 1 (O.S.)
          I smell something good.

                    PHILIPP
               (confused)
          Hello?

                    TROLL VOICE 2 (O.S.)
          A tasty treat.

Philipp brandishes his pistol in trepidation.

                    PHILIPP
          Come out, whoever you are. I'm
          armed.

                         TROLL VOICE 1 (O.S.)
                Want what's over fire? Or the
                morsel cooking it?

                         TROLL VOICE 2 (O.S.)
                Both.

CRACK! CRUNCH! Violent sounds erupt around Philipp as two
WOODLAND TROLLS reveal themselves.

Bits of rock and dirt fall from their fifteen-foot,
hunchbacked bodies: one with a boulder, the other a tree
stump.

                         PHILIPP
                Aaah!

Philipp stumbles back, shoots -- it ricochets off a troll.

He runs away.

EXT. FOREST GROVE - DAY

Philipp crouches behind trees obscuring a secluded pond where
young nude maidens, WATER NYMPHS, frolic among the lily pads.

                         PHILIPP (V.O.)
                The heart of every forest has
                secrets. Once I learned of one, I
                yearned to discover more.

He sneaks over to a clearing but sees only a swan. Philipp
creeps closer, stares at his own reflection.

A Nymph bursts from the water and pulls him in.

EXT. STEINAU - LAW OFFICE - DAY

Older now, Philipp wears a proper suit. He shakes hands with
another LAWYER in front of the respectable firm.

                         PHILIPP (V.O.)
                But leaving those supernatural
                pursuits proved to be more
                difficult than I expected.

EXT. FIELD - DAY

A bruised, disheveled Philipp hustles across an open prairie
wielding a rapier and pistol.

                         PHILIPP (V.O.)
                Some couldn't overlook past
                transgressions.

In the distance is a modest brick dwelling with a single
tower. He glances back at --

A pack of WEREWOLVES bearing down on him.

One werewolf gets close -- BAM! Not anymore.

EXT. EJJENSTEE CASTLE

Philipp scuttles through an overgrown courtyard of the
abandoned premises when another werewolf leaps from behind --

He thrusts his rapier out in defense, penetrating its
underbelly. A critical wound. Promptly withdraws the blade as
the animal reverts to a fetching WOMAN.

Philipp studies her face for a brief second, saddened by this
loss. Then escapes inside.

Werewolves soon arrive and congregate around the woman.

The ALPHA nudges its nose against her cheek. Transforms into
a middle-aged Baron who cradles his wife and cries.

INT. EJJENSTEE CASTLE - TOWER

Philipp drags himself up winding steps to the top. Locks the
door. Collapses in exhaustion.

HOWLING prompts a glance out the solitary window. Dismayed by
this predicament, he removes a leather-bound book and
portable brass inkwell from his satchel.

Philipp begins to write.

>   PHILIPP (V.O.)
>   The Weisse Frau will only bestow my
>   journal if needed...

The room becomes brighter until we fade to white.

INT. WATCH TOWER - CELLAR

Jacob finishes Philipp's final thought.

>   JACOB
>   For that, I'm sorry. This was never
>   the legacy I intended.

Dumbfounded.

>   MARIE
>   He'd still be proud.

82.

Jacob skims through the book: page after page filled with
illustrations and notes for trolls, weres, nymphs, spells...

                    JACOB
          Giants.

The page is blank except for a crude drawing and two words:

                    JACOB
               Easily provoked.

EXT. HELL'S VALLEY - DAY

Deep SNORES bellow. A riderless stallion trots along, reining
itself in near a trail.

Two BODILESS ARMS appear and gather rocks into a satchel
before vanishing.

Invisible Jacob hikes up the trail until he reaches a tree
overlooking MAGOG AND SIGENOT sleeping below. Skeletal
remains litter the ground like discarded food wrappers.

Rocks start pelting them. Magog snorts, brushes his nose.
Sigenot fidgets until a rock bounces off his eye.

He whacks Magog on the chest who jerks awake.

                    SIGENOT
               Stop knocking me.

                    MAGOG
               Idiot, I wasn't. Return to sleep.

Both giants resume their slumber until a larger stone hurls
from the tree and cracks across Sigenot's temple.

                    SIGENOT
               Why you hit?

                    MAGOG
               No ones hitting. You had a bad
               dream.

Magog wallops Sigenot upside the head.

                    SIGENOT
               That's no dream.

The giants stand, shoving, tempers rising.

                    MAGOG
               You're too stupid to know the
               difference.

                    SIGENOT
          Too bad!

Sigenot rips out a tree half his size and bashes Magog. Magog
clubs Sigenot across the face. An earth-shaking fight erupts!

EXT. BLACK FOREST - CHICKEN LEG HUT - SAME

The skull-topped wall keeps Marie at bay.

GLOWING EYES radiate out from GATEKEEPER SKULL, insolent with
a movable jaw.

                    GATEKEEPER SKULL
          No visitors.

                    MARIE
          Oh, a talking ornament. Grant me
          passage.

                    GATEKEEPER SKULL
          Foolish girl. Heed my warning. Baba
          Yaga serves up wrath to all
          trespassers.

She taps her blade on its chin.

                    MARIE
          I shall use you as a privy if
          denied.

                    GATEKEEPER SKULL
          Foul girl, enter at your own peril.

Two posts sink.

                    GATEKEEPER SKULL
          Expect to adorn this wall when
          she's finished.

INT. CHICKEN LEG HUT

Baba Yaga waits for Marie as though she were expected.

                    BABA YAGA
          Are you here by compulsion or free
          will?

Marie positions her sword in a fighting stance.

                    MARIE
          Does it matter?

84.

                    BABA YAGA
          Such a shame, child. I thought you
          wiser.

Two disembodied hands appear -- Marie chops them up with
quick precision.

                    MARIE
          Not wiser but definitely more
          skilled.

Baba Yaga's demeanor ruffles.

                    BABA YAGA
          There's nothing you possess I have
          not faced in 180 years.

                    MARIE
          Where is Jacob's brother?

                    BABA YAGA
          Gone from my sight.

                    MARIE
          Return him now, or your death will
          be slow and painful.

                    BABA YAGA
          Unlikely.
               (flicks her hand)
          Zomriet˘!

Nothing happens.

                    MARIE
          Disappointing.

Baba Yaga bum-rushes Marie who loses her sword. The witch
kicks it out of reach.

Marie knees Baba Yaga in the face.

                    BABA YAGA
          Wretched pest.

She spits out a bloody tooth. They wrestle to the floor.

EXT. HELL'S VALLEY

Both giants are bruised and bloody, wavering in their ability
to stay upright.

                    MAGOG
          Stop, stop dim--

THUNK! The killing stroke.

Magog drops like a sack of potatoes, kicking up a gust of air that blows through the tree.

                    SIGENOT
          Magog?

Sigenot pokes at his dead friend then sees Jacob's head.

                    SIGENOT
          Little mite!

He snatches Jacob and brings him up for closer inspection.

A bolt sails out from the void into Sigenot's eye.

The giant reels back, releasing Jacob --

Whose legs become exposed from the fluttering cloak before he lands on Magog's belly, rolls off, and runs --

Tripping over a pile of bones.

                    JACOB
          Honestly, make a better effort at
          discarding your remains.

He jiggles a rib cage off his foot.

Sigenot plucks the bolt like an eyelash.

Jacob hops onto the stallion and races away.

STOMP, STOMP, STOMP. Sigenot chases after him.

                    JACOB
          A familiar predicament.

Jacob veers up a mountain path, cutting through the forest at breakneck speed!

Sigenot demolishes trees in his frantic pursuit.

                    SIGENOT
          Come back here!

EXT. BLACK FOREST

Jacob advances on Gatekeeper Skull at full gallop.

                    GATEKEEPER SKULL
          No visitors!

The two posts spring back up. He clears them like an
equestrian rider.

INT. CHICKEN LEG HUT

Jacob disrupts a bizarre catfight between the women.

>   JACOB
>   She's not dead yet?

He rifles through Wilhelm's undisturbed clothing...

>   MARIE
>   Working on it. What delayed you?

She grabs Baba Yaga's hair, slams her face down.

>   JACOB
>   Complications arose.

...out pops a toad.

>   JACOB
>   Will!

>   MARIE
>   Will?

Baba Yaga smacks Marie off.

>   JACOB
>   One more is about to arrive.

KA-LACK. He points a flintlock pistol at the back of Baba
Yaga's head.

EXT. CHICKEN LEG HUT

Gatekeeper Skull freaks out...

>   GATEKEEPER SKULL
>   Noooooo!

...before Sigenot tramples through him.

Chicken Leg Hut bursts to life and flees from the oncoming
giant.

>   SIGENOT
>   Oooo, chicken.

INT. CHICKEN LEG HUT

Jacob's pistol misfires.

Everyone topples. The hut JOSTLES continually back and forth.

> BABA YAGA
> You brought a giant?!

She's unable to steady herself.

> BABA YAGA   SUBTITLE
> Dusˇa priatelia.   Soul friends.

Four disembodied hands materialize. They assist Baba Yaga
then attack Jacob.

He fights them off, wielding the malfunctioned flintlock like
a club.

> JACOB
> Marie! Kiss the toad!

> MARIE
> You kiss it!

> JACOB
> He'll change back. Trust me!

Marie stumbles around as she attempts to catch the hopping
amphibian.

> MARIE
> Has to quit moving first.

> JACOB
> Hurry awk--

Jacob claws at the disembodied hands strangling him.

Baba Yaga conjures the sword off her floor.

> BABA YAGA
> Enough of this.

Magically plunges it in Marie! She crumples. Everything
becomes muffled and distant.

Marie slowly peers down. Grabs the ivory handle protruding
from her stomach --

-- draws out the blade smeared in blood.

She wobbles to her feet. Musters a WAR CRY and impales Baba
Yaga!

All disembodied hands dissolve. Jacob doubles over, catching
his breath in spastic spurts.

Anchored to the wall, Baba Yaga squirms like a worm on a hook.

                    BABA YAGA
          Burrrrns, it burns.

                    MARIE
          I warned you. Slow and painful.

Jacob brings the toad to Marie. Winces at her injury.

                    JACOB
          How bad?

She hides the truth.

                    MARIE
          I'll manage.

The toad flicks its tongue out; Marie cringes in disgust.

                    MARIE
          He better thank me later.

                    JACOB
          With many lagers.

She kisses the toad --

                    JACOB
          Can't be!

                    MARIE
          Are you sure it's the right one?

                    JACOB
          How many others do you see?!

Baba Yaga snorts, cackles -- spits more blood.

                    BABA YAGA
          Poison cannot cure poison.

                    MARIE
          Speak in truth, soothsayer, no
          riddles.

She twists the sword, causing Baba Yaga to wail in new pain.

                    JACOB
          She did. What's the antidote for a
          kiss?

Marie COLDCOCKS Baba Yaga. Jacob has an epiphany.

He speaks to the toad.

                    JACOB
          I'm my brother's keeper.

Hurls it against the wall: POOF! Wilhelm materializes naked
and dazed...

                    WILHELM
          Was that really necessary?

...slowly fits on his discarded trousers and shirt.

                    JACOB
          He seems no worse for wear.

Jacob reaches for Marie. She doesn't budge, clothes soaked
through with blood down to her boot.

                    MARIE
              (shakes head)
          It's too late.

                    JACOB
          We can still find help.

                    MARIE
          I'm dying. Let me finish this.

                    JACOB
          I won't.

                    MARIE
          You must.

                    JACOB
          No! I love you!

Her eyes well up over his grief-stricken plea. She caresses
his cheek.

                    MARIE
          So much. Jacob, my love, I'll stay
          with you forever --

She touches his chest.

                    MARIE
          -- here. Live on for both of us.

They kiss for the last time.

EXT. BLACK FOREST - CHICKEN LEG HUT

The brothers jump off and take shelter in an oak tree hollow
just as --

Sigenot thunders past.

Chicken Leg Hut soars HIGH over a thick, impassable grove and
lands on the waterfall precipice, teetering...

INT. CHICKEN LEG HUT

The cauldron tips over: hot liquid splatters on Marie and
Baba Yaga, waking her.

                    BABA YAGA
          Your heroes have fled. The fairy
          tale is over.

                    MARIE
          After you wither and die.

                    BABA YAGA
               (choking chuckle)
          My race shall always be.

                    MARIE
          Death comes for us all, witch. I am
          yours... I am Death.

EXT. BLACK FOREST - WATERFALL

Sigenot's hulking mass flies through the air and crashes upon
the hut.

                    SIGENOT
        Got ya!

The cliff breaks away, plummets...

                    SIGENOT
        Aaaaaahhhhhhhh.

...smashing across the jagged rocks before flattened.

                  JACOB (V.O.)
        Thus ended Baba Yaga. She could not
        escape her past anymore than I.

Jacob and Wilhelm amble up to the edge.

                         JACOB (V.O.)
               Wilhelm became my one saving grace.
               How he survived remained a mystery,
               even to him. I can only surmise it
               was divine intervention.

They peer over at the devastation below.

Water splashes upon Sigenot's lifeless body before rejoining
the forest stream speckled by wood fragments floating away.

Among the debris is a periodic GLINT: maybe from a sword.

                         JACOB (V.O.)
               My anguish over Marie fueled a
               resurgence, welcomed by your
               father, in research and
               publication. Our lives devoted to
               making the falsehood a reality.

A single TEAR forms in his eye, slides down, and off --

INT. HUMBOLDT UNIVERSITY - CLASSROOM - DAY (1861)

-- blotting the parchment.

Jacob acquiesces his resurfaced emotions then continues.

                         JACOB (V.O.)
               Never again would I cherish more than
               my family, and the collective
               folklore of our great nation.

He closes next to the water spot:

                         JACOB (V.O.)
               With highest esteem, Jacob.

A moment of contemplation follows before Jacob inks the quill
and scribbles additional lines beneath his signature.

SUPERIMPOSE: "The Brothers Grimm went on to publish
                seven editions of *Children's and Household
                Tales*. Wilhelm married Henriette Wild and
                had four children. The first born was named
                Herman.

Jacob sprinkles pounce powder and folds the parchment. Drips
red wax until it pools into a GOOPY BLOB that he imprints
with the Grimm seal.

Letter in hand, Jacob eases himself off the chair. Shuffles
over to a back shelf...

                    JACOB (V.O.)
          PS. There's no reason to think
          monsters still lurk in our land,
          nor am I casting my mantle. The
          world has moved on.

...where the strongbox is tucked away.

He fishes the golden key out from under his shirt.

                    JACOB (V.O.)
          But do keep this disclosure
          protected for future generations.

The strongbox appears empty.

Jacob sweeps "air" aside to expose the preserved   leather-
bound book and places his letter on top.

                    JACOB (V.O.)
          One can never predict when such
          knowledge may be requisite.

                                        FADE OUT.

ABOUT THE SCREENWRITER

Michael E. Berg is an acclaimed screenwriter and award-winning producer who graduated from the University of Northern Iowa. Start a Shakespeare authorship debate with him @writtenbyberg or spilledinkcinema.com. Michael continues to reside in central Iowa with his wife and three children.

120pages

EXPOSURE. CREDIBILITY. PROFIT.

PUBLISH YOUR SCREENPLAY WITH **120pages**!

You've spent countless hours — maybe years — writing your screenplay. You believe it in it, but it has not yet been picked up for production.

By publishing your screenplay with 120pages, you will:

- Earn income from your work
- Give your screenplay exposure
- Build your credibility as a screenwriter

Visit **120pages.com** today to learn more!